Metal screamed on asphalt as the truck tipped on its side

The noise was an overwhelming assault on Gadgets's hearing. Finally it stopped. But the firing continued, the Syrian ambushers ripping into the wreck with autoweapons.

Throwing open a door, Gadgets saw the Syrians firing from the protection of a stone wall. Slugs hammered into the overturned truck.

"This is serious! Pol, you ready to get out of here?"

"I'm tangled in gear," Pol Blancanales yelled as Gadgets ducked back under cover. "Put out some rounds!"

Seizing his Colt Commando, Gadgets rose again and fired bursts of alternating tracer and hollowpoint slugs out of the door.

That was when he saw a Syrian stand up behind the wall with a rocket launcher. He sighted on the guy and pulled the trigger. But just as his tracers found the Syrian, the rocket launcher sprayed fire.

Gadgets stared end-on at the onrushing warhead.

Then the rocket hit the truck.

Mack Bolan's
ABLE TEAM

ABLE TEAM
Rain of Doom

Dick Stivers

A GOLD EAGLE BOOK FROM
W🌐RLDWIDE

TORONTO · NEW YORK · LONDON · PARIS
AMSTERDAM · STOCKHOLM · HAMBURG
ATHENS · MILAN · TOKYO · SYDNEY

First edition February 1985

ISBN 0-373-61216-8

Special thanks and acknowledgment to
G. H. Frost for his contributions to this work.

Printed in Canada

1

Pulling the tab on a can of orange soda, Gadgets Schwarz watched the glass towers of Miami reflect the red dawn. As the Air Force jet climbed and took a southwest course, he inspected the gray landscape. Patterns of lights marked towns. Lines of lights—blue-white streetlights and amber headlights—defined roads. He saw Route 41 to the north. Then the jet left the suburbs and roads behind for the forest and grass-lands of the Everglades.

"Forget the sight-seeing," said Jack Grimaldi, coming from the pilot's cabin. "Tonight you got reservations on a fast boat to the People's Republic of Nicaragua. There'll be lots of friends for you to meet, a beach party, fireworks."

"What are you talking about?" Gadgets asked. A veteran of the Green Berets and the electronics specialist for Able Team, he eyed the stack of folders carried by the man behind Grimaldi.

"It'll be a surprise party for an Iranian. This is George. He'll tell you what goes."

Gray-haired, overweight, in his forties, George looked like the stereotypical officer of the bureaucracy. Decades of worry had lined his face, which was unshaven this morning; his gray suit was years out of style. He passed a folder of maps and photocopies and photos to Gadgets.

Rosario Blancanales, an American of Puerto Rican heritage and another veteran of the Green Berets, shook hands with the bureaucrat. "It's a pleasure to meet you, George. Looks like we woke you up early today."

"I haven't slept for days," George said, handing Blancanales a folder.

"So what's going on?" Gadgets persisted.

"Just a minute. George'll brief you," Grimaldi answered.

Carl Lyons, the blond ex-Los Angeles Police Department detective, was lying on a couch at the back of the plane. He did not move as Grimaldi and George approached.

Grimaldi reached down to shake Lyons, but Lyons's hand closed around the other man's wrist first.

"Let me sleep," said the ex-detective, not opening his eyes.

"Get with it, hotshot. No time to dream. You got studying to do before Nicaragua."

Lyons rose instantly. Releasing Grimaldi's arm, he took the folder George offered. He looked at the first page, an eight-by-ten black-and-white print.

"Who's this guy?" Lyons asked.

"An Iranian. Colonel Ali Dastgerdi of the Syrian army," George answered. He closed the plastic window shades as he returned to the front of the plane, then dimmed the interior lights and hit a switch. A screen automatically rolled down as a projector's fan whirred.

"But if he's Iranian," Blancanales asked, pointing to the grainy black-and-white photo in his folder, "why is he with the Syrians?"

"That's one of the questions we want to ask him," George replied as he pressed a button. "This is Dastgerdi."

Several slides of the Iranian flashed on the screen in succession. In two, he appeared in the uniform of the Syrian army. In others, he wore civilian clothes.

"He was the commander of Aziz Rouhani, an Iranian you already know."

On the screen appeared the bearded, thick-featured face of an Iranian peasant staring at the camera, his face deathly white against the black of his beard.

"Hey, there he is!" Gadgets laughed. "How's he getting along since the Ironman did the double zap on him?"

"Not well. Not well at all."

Gadgets and Lyons laughed.

"What's the joke?" Grimaldi asked. "You jokers fucked up in Mexico. Now you got to go—"

"Fucked up?" Gadgets asked, incredulous. "We left those losers in flames, burning! Nothing left but ashes."

Weeks before, Able Team had pursued a gang of Iranian Revolutionary Guards from Beirut to Mexico City. There, Able joined forces with elite antiterrorist commandos of the Mexican army to confront a Soviet conspiracy promising peace, but plotting death not only to Able Team but, inexplicably, also to the Iranian terrorists. Outmaneuvering and destroying the KGB agents and Mexican gangsters, Able Team raced north to encircle and destroy the Iranians and their trucks of Soviet rockets.

"Yes, you wiped them out," George agreed. "But we think they were only a decoy."

"What?" Blancanales demanded. "I can't believe that! They had rockets. They had planes and trucks. They—"

"And those black-nationalist freaks," Lyons added.

"The Iranians and crazies," Blancanales continued, "were an organized unit ready to go north and hit the President. When the trucks burned, I saw those rockets go off."

"No doubt about it," Gadgets added. "They were the real thing."

"The real thing was in the Bekaa Valley," George said.

"In Lebanon?" Blancanales asked.

"Then turn the plane around!" Lyons shouted. "Forget Costa Rica—"

"Dastgerdi is in Nicaragua!" George spoke over Able Team. "Here!"

He pushed the slide-advance button, and the three men went quiet. A shoreline appeared on the screen: a wide, swampy river flowing into a bay sheltered by a long tongue of land; a line of hills overlooked the river and bay.

Docks and freighters filled the bay. A compound with roads, buildings and long rectangular warehouses lined the shore. Between the compound and the hills, a shantytown followed the wavering line of a creek.

"Finally," George whispered to Grimaldi in an aside. "Are these clowns actually professionals?"

"Only way to shut them up is to give them a target. It's your show. Take over." Grimaldi returned to the pilot's compartment.

George pointed to the harbor complex. "La Laguna de Perlas, Nicaragua. A major public-works project by the new people's government. Soviet freighters, Soviet floating docks, Soviet prefab warehouses, Soviet prefab barracks. Note the chain link and concertina wire enclosing the complex. Our sources report that no one enters or leaves without clearance. Our sources also report there are no—I repeat, no—workers from the surrounding villages. No local people. Only outsiders sent from Managua and ComBloc technicians."

His hand traced a line leading west. "This all-weather highway carries weapons, munitions and heavy vehicles, such as tanks and armored cars, to the interior. As far as we have been able to determine, the government of Nicaragua established this harbor solely for the offloading of Soviet weapons."

George pointed to a long white strip south of the bay. "You will go ashore on this beach. Here, in this lighthouse, is a bunker guarding the entrance to the harbor. Sandinista regulars—repeat, regular forces, not the militia of teenage draftees—patrol the beach, the hills and the village on foot and in vehicles. There are also patrols in boats and sometimes in light aircraft.

"After landing, you will cross this stretch of flat ground and go over this ridge. Here—" the bureaucrat pointed to the winding stream passing through the southern end of the compound "—is a culvert. Our people report that storms have washed out the alarms. This will be your point of entry.''

"And what if it isn't the way you say?'' Lyons asked.

"It will be.''

"Who will be our liaison?'' Blancanales asked.

"A group of Miskito Indians. Members of a force that mounts frequent incursions into the region's coastal facilities.''

Lyons pressed his question. "What happens if it isn't like you say?''

"I suggest you closely study the information the Agency prepared. You will see you have considerable resources with which to counter any contingency.''

"Like what?''

"Oh, wow!'' Gadgets exclaimed, looking up from the photocopied pages in his folder. "A multiband coded frequency-impulse transmitter. Far fucking out! Forget you, Ironman. I don't need you this time. I'll take my magic box in all by myself.''

"What is a multiband—'' Blancanales started.

Gadgets continued to read from the list. "Ah...you will be going, after all. I'll need someone to carry claymores.''

"Claymores? How many?''

"Ten or fifteen.''

"What? You'll break my back with that—''

"Ironman, you can do it. Three and a half pounds each. No problem. Not for a big mean man like you.''

"That's forty-something pounds—''

George interrupted them. "You three men have five hours only to prepare. I have been with this project since you captured Rouhani. If you have questions, only I can answer them. And nothing in those folders leaves this aircraft. This project is classified Top Secret, Need to Know Only—''

"And Burn Before Reading," Lyons interrupted. "I got a question already. Dastgerdi's in Nicaragua—so what? If the rockets are in Lebanon, why aren't we going there?"

"We do not know that the rockets are in fact still in the Bekaa Valley," George answered. "The rockets may be in transit or they may have already arrived in Nicaragua. But we know for certain as of yesterday that Dastgerdi's in La Laguna de Perlas. Interrogating him will reveal if the rockets are there, or if—"

Blancanales spoke next. "And what if they are not?"

"Hopefully, the information we gain from Dastgerdi will allow us to intercept them on the Atlantic."

"Hopefully?" Lyons demanded. "What does that mean? We can't hope for shit. What happens if—"

The screen went black. George flicked on the lights. "The briefing is over. Study your materials. I repeat, nothing leaves this—"

"Hey, clerk! I'm asking a question!" Lyons shouted. "You said you've been on this for weeks. So what happens if the rockets aren't in Nicaragua or on a ship? I'll tell you what happens! We'll go to Lebanon and hit those ragheads like we should've as soon as you found out we got played by a decoy. And I want to know what you desk jockeys have been doing for all these weeks!"

"Ixnay," Gadgets snapped. "He looks like he's been working."

Blancanales seconded the question. "I believe my

partner has a valid point. When the Agency learned that we had failed to complete our mission, why weren't we immediately dispatched to hit the real threat?''

"Any project of this kind requires intensive consultation and coordination between offices. Matters of international policy and diplomacy—''

Lyons cut him off with a sneer. "Talk or take a walk, Mr. George the Clerk. I asked a question. Answer it.''

"Do you believe," George answered, his face suddenly red with anger, "that you make this government's international policy?''

"Forget the foreign-policy jive. We know what goes on. And we know what we've got to do.''

"Do you believe that you. . . cowboy mercenaries can continue improvising your way through one adventure after another, destroying years of subtle diplomacy for the sadistic thrills of your death-squad antics? I will tell you this. The value of your team is under debate. And actions such as your complete disregard of the order to arrest Powell in Beirut do not enhance your prospects for continued employment.''

"So that's what took so long," Lyons said, nodding. "That's what took you clerks weeks. You knew about the rockets. But you had to debate whether to send us.''

"Your team is wildly erratic in the performance of your assignments.''

"We get the job done. We do what's necessary. Now, you—'' Lyons left his seat and advanced on the middle-aged bureaucrat. Blancanales grabbed Lyons's arm.

"Calm down.''

"You will get out of my sight. Because my instincts are telling me—''

"Be cool!" Gadgets shouted at Lyons. "You throw him out, it'll depressurize the cabin and my orange pop here will most definitely lose its fizz. So be cool!"

George retreated into the pilot's cabin. Seconds later, Grimaldi stepped out. He scanned the seats. The three men of Able Team were reading the prepared materials.

"What's going on back here?"

Gadgets looked at his partners. He looked to the back of the passenger cabin. He looked up at the ceiling. He looked under his seat. "Nothing's going on. You see anything going on?"

"If nothing's going on," Grimaldi asked, suppressing a grin, "how come our friend George is hiding up front? You guys keep aggravating the Agency clerks, you just might not get any more of these all-expense-paid trips to faraway exotic countries. Understand? Wouldn't have the pleasure of hunting down international creeps and stepping on them. To make the world a better place to live."

Lyons grinned. "Well, then maybe we'd just hang around Washington, D.C., and step on a few Georgie boys. Wouldn't that make the world a better place to live?"

2

Rain beat down on their backs. Wind-driven waves splashed into the inflated boat. Leaning over plastic oars, Able Team and their Miskito *contra* allies rowed for the harbor of La Laguna de Perlas, on the Caribbean coast of Nicaragua.

The Miskito *contras*, descendants of the indigenous peoples of Central America, accompanied Able Team as contract soldiers—mercenaries. They would invest the thousands of dollars Able Team paid for this night raid in their continuing war against the Sandinistas. Like their ancestors who fought the Spanish Conquistadors, the young soldiers from northeast Nicaragua fought for the survival of their culture. In the sixties and seventies, they fought the fascist Somoza regime's attempts to seize their lands. Now they fought the tyranny of the Soviet Sandinistas, who had initiated a program of forced collectivization of the Miskito tribes.

For Miskitos, tonight's raid represented only one more skirmish in a centuries-old struggle.

North of the dinghy, two red beacons flashed, marking the entrance to the harbor. When the plastic boat rose on a swell, the scattered lights of the town became visible. But in the darkness and falling rain, nothing of the shore could be seen.

The six men aboard the tiny dinghy heard waves breaking. Without a word, they rowed deeper and faster. The time of greatest danger was upon them. Upon the open water, their black-suited forms and black boat concealed by the night, they faced little chance of being spotted by the Sandinistas. But in the white foam of the breaking waves or on the pale sand of the beach, a sharp-eyed sentry might easily see them and sound the alarm.

A swell lifted the boat. Groaning with the exertion, all six men pulled in unison. The swell passed, then broke a few meters ahead. They drove the oars down again and pulled hard. Another swell lifted the boat. The men pulled their oars through the water in unison.

The boat flexed as the wave crested, then shot toward the beach, skipping over backwash. White foam engulfed the men. Blinded by the churning water, they continued toward the beach.

When they neared the sand, two men dashed toward the wind-whipped palms, pulling the dinghy. The three members of Able Team and a Miskito, a teenager who moved with the calm and efficiency of a career soldier, removed the heavy gear from the boat. The Miskito teenager stayed with the boat. Gadgets, Blancanales and Lyons grunted across the beach to join the two lookouts. Then the lookouts advanced into the palms.

Able Team waited, weapons in hand, packs of munitions and electronics on their backs. Warm rain streamed down their faces and fatigues. Blancanales looked back and saw the oval shadow of another boat in the breaking waves. He nudged his partners.

"That's number two," Gadgets whispered.

"There's number three." Lyons pointed a hundred

meters to the south. Two dark forms sprinted from the waves to the palms.

Three boats had left the cruiser offshore. Able Team, laden with equipment, needed the help of three Miskito soldiers. The two other boats each carried four men.

In seconds, the lookouts sent an all-clear code on their radios. The men at the boats dragged the inflated crafts into the palms and camouflaged them with palm fronds and brush, then returned to the shore with branches and whisked away the marks of the boats and every bootprint.

Able Team unpacked and distributed equipment. Two *contras* and the sentries who would remain with the boats received Pocketscopes. The passive night sights used second-generation image-intensification electronics to amplify the ambient light of the stars and moon.

As the Miskitos checked the scopes, Blancanales switched on the NVS-700 Starlite scope fitted to his M-16/M-203 over-and-under assault rifle/grenade launcher. He scanned the darkness, the light-amplification electronics turning the rainy night to brilliant green-and-white day. Then he slipped a suppressor over the muzzle of the M-16 and jammed in a magazine of Interdynamics reduced-charge 5.56mm cartridges. Though Blancanales, Gadgets and Lyons all carried silenced pistols, the combination of the Starlite and Interdynamics suppressor kit gave them the capability of invisible, silent attack over a range of two hundred meters.

Gadgets checked the multifrequency coded impulse

generator. Tonight, though he would not even carry a rifle, he had the greatest responsibility. The Sandinistas had garrisoned hundreds of soldiers in the region: the satellite photos revealed barracks near the workshops and docks of the harbor. If a sentry or guard dog saw Able Team slip into town, the latter risked pursuit by a battalion of Nicaraguan soldiers commanded by Cuban and Soviet officers. Gadgets could not stop a battalion with the electronics and radio-triggered claymores he carried, but he could slow one down. Other than his heavy gear, he carried only a knife and a silenced Beretta 93-R.

Impatient, Lyons waited for the others, his eyes piercing the darkness. He carried his standard equipment: a four-inch Colt Python in a shoulder holster, a modified-for-silence Colt Government Model and a Konzak selective-fire 12-gauge assault shotgun. He had no faith in electronics, only in firepower.

"Ready to go," Gadgets whispered. He passed Lyons a backpack. Lyons shouldered it and stood, the weight of his weapons, ammunition and twenty kilos of explosive and steel forcing him to stoop. The pack contained ten of Gadgets's claymore mines and a reserve multifrequency transmitter.

Led by one of the young *contras* who scanned the darkness with a night viewer, they moved along the beach. Wind thrashed the palms, covering the noise of their boots on the sand. Three times Gadgets stopped to lash claymores to the trees.

Beacon lights marked the entry to the lagoon, a kilometer-long spit of low hills and palms designed by East German engineers to create a harbor for freight-

ers and patrol boats. The beacon on the eastern side
was mounted on a steel tower. On the western side,
where a steep hill descended almost to the beach, the
beacon sat on a two-story concrete building. Gunports
overlooked the lagoon and the passage into the Caribbean.

Looking through the night viewer, one of the Miskitos spotted two sentries. They stood in the building,
scanning the storm-whipped ocean with binoculars.
The *contra* pointman went flat in the sand and motioned Blancanales forward.

Rain streaming off his eyebrows, he watched
shadows pace inside the beacon house. The revolution
of the beacon light illuminated the night in a sweeping
section of diffuse red. When the light beamed toward
him, Blancanales saw nothing. When it beamed away,
the soft red of the falling rain backlit the sentries in the
beacon house. He saw three of them.

Replacing the caps on his Starlite scope, Blancanales
crawled back to his partners. "No problem...."

Leaving the beach, they cut inland along a trail
evidently used by patrols. Gadgets positioned another
claymore. The trail twisted up the hill. As they approached the ridge, the pointman went flat and crept
forward. A minute passed. Then the pointman motioned them on.

The ridge had been cleared of palms and brush. To
the east, at the end of the ridge, was the beacon house.
To the west, the naked ridge vanished into the night.
To the north was the village and harbor.

Only poor fishermen and their families lived in La
Laguna, no more than a line of shacks and a dirt road

along a rain-flooded creek. But two hundred meters away, on the other side of a chain-link fence and security lights, Cuban and ComBloc advisors enjoyed the modern comforts of the harbor complex.

Prefabricated barracks housed the Cubans and ComBloc nationals. Diesel generators provided electricity to light the barracks, offices and warehouses near the piers. On three long piers, lit as bright as day by mercury-arc lamps, Able Team saw pairs of sentries in black plastic raincoats patrolling.

Despite the storm, a freighter with deck-mounted cranes was being unloaded. Workmen in bright yellow rain slickers attached cables to cargo containers, which were being hoisted onto diesel trucks with flatbed trailers on the dock.

Blancanales pointed to the junction of the creek and the lagoon. Then he traced the creek through the harbor-complex fence. Exactly as the anti-Soviet agents in La Laguna had described and as satellite photography had confirmed, the flooding creek provided an entry to the harbor facilities.

"The clerk got it right," Lyons admitted.

As the others surveyed the harbor, Gadgets placed three more claymores. He worked by the intermittent red glow of the beacon light, carefully positioning the claymores, then securing them to immovable backstops: a jutting rock, a palm stump, a rotting palm tree. When he finished, he crept back to the group.

"How many left in your pack?" Lyons whispered to him.

"Down to three."

"Then take some of mine."

"No way. Those are for down there." Gadgets pointed to the harbor complex. "Couldn't sort them out in the dark."

"What're you talking about? Just take five of them."

"And scramble the sequence? Forget it! You don't want to mess with the sequence."

Blancanales motioned Lyons forward. The Puerto Rican, a veteran of twenty years of war, pointed to a ridge less than a hundred meters from the fence. "I'm leaving one of our friends on that hillside there with this rifle and Starlite." He tapped the M-16/M-203 he carried.

"And two men at the fence?"

"No. He can cover us. The other goes with us."

Lyons nodded. One at a time, the men went downhill through the flowing mud as the rain splashed down. They reached the flooding stream minutes later.

Stripping off his bandolier of 5.56mm magazines and six 40mm grenades, Blancanales passed his M-16/M-203 to one of the *contras*. The teenager took it and climbed the hill to a point where he could cover their entry and exit.

They continued to the fence in single file, fighting the current and drifting debris. Where the stream passed under the fence was a tangle of branches and litter. The force of the surging water had bent the chain-link fence. Though the security lights illuminated the area, no one inside the complex or patrolling the perimeter could see the infiltrators in the stream.

Blancanales directed two of the young *contras* to the

banks, one to each side: they crawled to the top and watched for patrols. Then Lyons and the *contras* ripped into the tangle, pulling fronds aside, dragging branches clear. Lyons found a piece of lumber jammed in the streambed. He stood on the board and gripped the chain link.

Breaking the board, Lyons released the entire mass of debris. Gadgets grabbed Lyons's feet. Blancanales and a teenage *contra* clutched at the bank. Another *contra* lost his footing and disappeared: Lyons saw him reappear, choking and sputtering, twenty meters past the fence. He immediately scrambled to the bank. Staying low, he swam back to the others, remaining hidden in the shadows.

One by one they ducked under the rushing black water. Lyons held the fence until the others had gone under, then dropped. The two lookouts went last.

Between the stream and the barracks were parked trucks and stacks of crated cargo. Grinning, Lyons passed the heavy pack of claymores to Gadgets. Then he tightly cinched the sling of his Konzak, binding the assault shotgun against his body, and slipped out his modified-for-silence Colt. Blancanales and Gadgets worked the actions of their silenced Beretta 93-R autopistols.

Lyons, followed by a *contra* with a machete, dashed to a truck's trailer and went flat beside the wheels. Rainwater streaming from the truck's plastic-covered cargo poured over their muddy blacksuits. Lyons motioned for the *contra* to wait, then snaked toward the barracks. He crept across an open stretch of mud and hid behind another parked truck.

Looking across a two-lane asphalt road illuminated by mercury-arc lamps, he saw garages and workshops. Another asphalt lane separated the utility buildings from the barracks.

Where the road met the dock, a group of soldiers stood at a sandbagged machine-gun position. In the opposite direction, toward the gate of the complex, two soldiers paced the fence.

Lyons took the hand-radio from his belt, clicked down the transmit, and whispered, "We can't cross the road."

"Look for another way," Blancanales told him.

"There isn't...unless.... Stand by."

Staying flat in the mud, Lyons crawled alongside two heavy diesel trucks, a tractor, an ancient Chevrolet pickup and a ComBloc flatbed truck. Then he approached an old Dodge panel truck. He scanned the vehicles around him, scanned the road. He saw no one. Rising, he tried the door.

The foul scent of alcohol filled his nostrils. As his eyes adjusted to the dark interior, he heard snoring come from the back. Seeing a man curled on the floor, Lyons holstered his modified Colt.

He pushed the seat forward and lunged inside. He tore away the man's shirt, jammed it into his mouth and threw the suddenly awakened drunk onto his face. Lyons took plastic riot handcuffs from his web belt and secured the man's hands. An oily rag went around the drunk's head as a blindfold. Finding the keys to the Dodge in the drunk's pocket, he clicked on his hand-radio.

"I got transportation."

Minutes later, as the others crowded into the truck, Blancanales put the prisoner's jacket over his blacksuit. Then he drove directly to the building where the Iranian allegedly slept.

The Nicaraguan Communists had provided first-class quarters for their visiting comrades. Unlike the technicians and shipping crews who stayed in the barracks, the ComBloc officers enjoyed private suites and conference rooms. Their one-story bungalows boasted patios and landscaping.

Able Team knew the numbers of the rooms occupied by the Iranian and his group. Blancanales stopped the truck at the Iranian's bungalow. As the *contras* checked their weapons, Lyons said to Blancanales, "Remind them that our targets are the Soviets and Iranians. They don't get paid extra for killing Nicaraguans."

Gadgets laughed softly. "Mercy for the Sandinistas? That don't sound like the blood-lusting, Commie-hating Ironman we know and love."

"What? I just don't want them wasting time making numbers for a body count. We're here for information."

"Oh. Ironman the efficient."

As Blancanales spoke to the Miskito *contras* in idiomatic Spanish, Gadgets prepared claymores for placement. Lyons glanced to the shadowed doors of the bungalows. He screwed valved hearing protectors into his ears.

In a split second, Lyons, Blancanales and four *contras* were out of the Dodge. In pairs, they went to three doors. Three kicks sounded and three doors sprang open simultaneously.

Behind them, Gadgets moved silently through the rain, placing claymores. He made no effort at concealment. In a few seconds, the alarms would sound.

Rushing through a bungalow, the modified-for-silence Colt in his hands, Lyons heard glass shatter. He kicked open the bedroom door and spun to one side as a pistol fired wild. He called out, "White light! *Luce blanco—*"

The *contra* pitched in a stun-shock grenade. Designed for antiterrorist confrontations, the grenade had no shrapnel. It exploded with a deafening blast and a blinding flash.

In the other rooms, stun-shocks boomed. A pistol fired, then two more grenades exploded.

Not moving, a dark-haired, narrow-faced semitic man groaned in bed, his eyes fluttering. Then he collapsed onto the sheets. Lyons cinched plastic handcuffs around his wrists and ankles while the *contra* teenager gathered his papers. Lyons buckled a nylon harness around the prisoner's shoulders, waist and feet. The harness had loops providing handholds for carrying.

The papers in his wallet provided an identity: Ahmed Choufi, a Syrian with an international import-export company.

Jerking Choufi off the bed, Lyons dragged him through the broken glass. In the other rooms, autofire hammered.

Returning to consciousness, Choufi pleaded for his life, first in French and Arabic, then English. "I am no one, only a businessman.... Why do you do this?"

"Shut up or you get a bullet," Lyons ordered.

"But I am no one political."

Dragging his prisoner into the rain, Lyons kneed him in the gut. Gasping, choking, the Syrian struggled to breathe. An AK-47 flashed from the end of the lane, slugs slamming into the bungalow. Lyons saw Gadgets brace his silent Beretta 93-R with both hands. The pistol recoiled once. Someone in the darkness cried out. The rifleman didn't fire again.

Blancanales, emerging from the bungalows alone, whispered to Lyons, "He wasn't there! No clothes, no luggage, nothing!"

Lifting his prisoner's head by an ear, Lyons demanded, "Where's Dastgerdi? Where is he?"

"Who?"

Lyons aimed his silenced Colt at the Syrian's left foot.

Choufi begged, "No more! Have mercy! I know nothing of the colonel's affairs."

"Where is he?"

"He returned to Syria today."

"If he's here, you live. If not, you die. Where is he?"

"Have mercy!" Choufi lapsed into Arabic.

The two *contras* from the third bungalow rushed to Blancanales and spoke rapidly in Spanish, handing him a folder of identification papers. Blancanales nodded and sent the men to the truck.

Several Sandinista militiamen ran to the bungalows. One staggered as a silent 9mm slug punched into his chest; then bursts from the *contras'* M-16 rifles dropped the others.

"Christ, it's gone wrong!" the Puerto Rican cursed. "They had an accident. Their man opened up on them and they killed him, blew off his head. . . ."

Lyons thought fast. "Wizard! Here, fast! Bring a radio-pop. And one of those dead men. A skinny one. We got to improvise."

"What?" Blancanales asked.

"It's a sixty-six percent failure so far. Let's make it one hundred percent."

"What are you talking about?"

Snapping open Choufi's briefcase, Lyons removed the Syrian's identification. Gadgets and a *contra* carried a thin, bloody, dead militiaman.

"I don't even want to know what you're doing with that," Gadgets jived.

"Get that radio-pop ready." Lyons glanced at the dead man: a bearded, hard-muscled, middle-aged soldier, punctured by a crescent of 5.56mm slugs. His height and weight approximated the Syrian's. Lyons jerked the corpse off the walkway, dragged it into the bungalow and threw it onto the bed.

"Cut off his gear and uniform and boots. Put the claymore on his head."

"What?"

"I want nothing left of him except a stain."

"That's what he'll be."

As Gadgets stripped the dead man, Lyons found the Syrian's slacks and pocketed his identification. He kicked the slacks across the room.

Seconds later, they sprinted into the rain. Autofire came from both ends of the street. The *contras* returned fire with their M-16 rifles, Blancanales with his silent Beretta. Lyons and Gadgets dived into a muddy flower bed.

From the ends of the street, the muzzles of Kalashni-

kov rifles flashed. From doorways and corners, militiamen raked the intruders with full-auto fire.

AK slugs roared over the North Americans to shatter the bungalow windows, hammer the walls. A hail
of 7.62mm ComBloc slugs punched through the
stolen Dodge and whined away. Shattered glass fell
around them. Gadgets surveyed the street, noting the
positions of the Sandinistas. He shouted to the *contras, "¡Mata las luces!"* He pointed to the streetlights.

"¡Inmediatamente!" one teenager answered.

Shifting their aim from the Sandinistas, the *contras*
plinked out the lights one by one. Globes shattered,
darkened, the crashing sound loud even amid the
cacophony of shouts and shooting and whining slugs.

High above, on the third floor of the barracks, a
silhouette appeared, a pistol popped from a window—
fatal mistake. Three *contras* sighted and fired. The
silhouette disappeared.

Gadgets surveyed the dark street. He called, "Ready
to go?"

"Quinze segundos." Several voices answered.

He turned to Lyons. "Watch this magic trick."

Flipping open his multiband impulse transmitter,
the Able Team electronics specialist laughed as he
keyed a series of digital codes. "Now you see
them...."

Simultaneous explosions ripped the darkness in one
shattering crack of C-4. A sound like hundreds of fly-
ing bullets followed as a storm of steel pellets penetrated the distance, shattering glass, bouncing off
steel, imbedding in wood, rattling on sheet metal.

The return fire had died. In silence, the *contras* and North Americans dragged their prisoner into the panel truck. Brushing glass and plastic shards off the seat, Blancanales turned on the ignition and accelerated away.

"Take the same way out as we came in," Gadgets shouted. "That way's got the radio-pops."

"Hit the button on the bedroom!" Lyons told Gadgets.

"Ain't safe," Gadgets answered. "Gotta wait until we're around the corner."

With the muzzle of his Konzak, Lyons smashed what remained of the windshield. He jerked back the actuator to chamber the first 12-gauge round. But he saw no targets.

Skidding around the corner, they saw the effect of Gadgets's radio-detonated claymores. Where a group of militiamen had been firing from the barracks, only rags and torn flesh remained. Vast streams of blood flowed from headless, limbless corpses. The volleys of steel pellets had denuded the grounds of landscaping, shattered every window, punched hundreds of holes in the barracks.

Gadgets keyed another code. Another blast shook the night. "I declare that guy gone."

Roaring through the complex, they encountered other headlights. Militiamen were running in all directions. In the confusion, no one fired at the speeding truck. Lyons, low in the seat, kept his Konzak ready. Gadgets, looking back, saw the living gather around the dead. A few rifle shots resounded from inside the bungalows.

Blancanales maneuvered the Dodge between a large truck and a cargo container in the storage area, parking behind a stack of telephone poles. As the others dragged out the Syrian, Blancanales braced his silenced Beretta on the poles and methodically extinguished the lights along the security perimeter. In the distance, the one-sided firefight continued.

They ran through the darkness to the stream, which was swelled by the rain. As they carried the bound-and-gagged Syrian through the rushing water, sudden glare lit them.

Waiting for the *contra* teenager to transport the prisoner across the fence, Lyons and Gadgets did not move. High above them, a magnesium flare swung on a miniature parachute. They saw two jeeps of Sandinista militiamen speed from the complex. Spotlights followed the jeeps along the fence.

"Time to shortstop the pursuit," Gadgets told Lyons. He pointed to a small rectangle visible by the flare's light twenty meters away, hanging on the side of an aluminum shipping container.

"See that?"

"Yeah. A claymore?"

"Absolutely right! That's the pop covering this area." He keyed a series of numbers into the impulse transmitter. "What if I'd taken some of those claymores out of your pack? What if I'd gotten the sequence scrambled? You understand? Like what if I pressed the button—"

He touched a digital key. At once, all the claymores planted throughout the harbor complex exploded. Fragments of steel sprayed the two jeeps: their headlights went black and they lurched to a standstill on flat tires. Flames spread as gasoline spilled. Nothing moved in the wrecks.

"What if I pressed the button and that one—" Gadgets indicated a claymore only a few steps away "—went off instead of those others? You understand?"

"No doubt about it. I understand."

"Technology's great," Gadgets jived, closing the impulse transmitter. "But you got to keep it straight."

The flare sputtered out. Gadgets and Lyons slipped under the flowing water and escaped into the darkness.

3

In a chrome-and-plastic lounge of Orly international airport, Colonel Dastgerdi of the Syrian army waited. The casual sports clothes he wore had been purchased in a Madrid men's shop. His lightweight headphones lulled him with a Spanish pop ballad. Surreptitiously he watched the entrances, studying the face of every passenger who emerged from the terminal.

Two days earlier he had flown from Managua to Madrid. After a few hours' delay, he continued to Paris, and there spent a night in a luxurious hotel, enjoying the French cuisine and an expensive Vietnamese prostitute. Recalling the pleasures of that evening, he consulted his wristwatch. In a few minutes he would be departing on another long flight. Destination: Damascus.

A man approached, also wearing the lightweight headphones of a portable cassette player. His nondescript Semitic features and cheap clothing—a gray sport coat and gray slacks—made him appear like a poor, grubby, foreign laborer, one of thousands in Europe. The portable cassette player enhanced the image of the hardworking Arab returning home to the distant East with his savings and a few luxuries after a year's work in the West. Dastgerdi looked elsewhere as the man crossed the lounge and sat beside him.

In Arabic the man asked, "What are you listening to?"

Dastgerdi pulled the tape player from his coat pocket and ejected the cassette. "See?"

The man took the cassette, looked at the label. "I don't read Spanish." Passing it back, he took another from his pocket. "You might like this. Play it when you are home."

It was pocketed. Though the case bore the label of a Swedish singing group, the tape carried digital information that could be decoded only by an American desk-top computer, like the one in Dastgerdi's Damascus office.

A United Nations diplomat had purchased several of the small computers from an ordinary electronics shop in New York City. They were shipped as diplomatic papers to Moscow. Then Soviet technicians modified and reprogrammed them to serve as coding machines. Their outward appearance remained unchanged. Though the codes they created would not withstand the scrutiny of the American National Security Agency or the Soviet KGB, the codes did deny outsiders access to Dastgerdi's communications. And the cassettes, appearing to contain only music, would pass by customs inspectors without difficulty.

"Any other information?" Dastgerdi asked.

His companion glanced at the predominantly European passengers around them, who would be seeing only two Middle Easterners chatting about music before their respective flights. Then he spoke in a low voice.

"Fascist *contras* hit the port. Choufi is dead,

Gabriel is dead. But there has been no compromise of the mission. The Nicaraguans drove away the fascists and annihilated them in the mountains.''

The news seemed to disrupt Dastgerdi's equanimity; in fact, only by the strength of his years of training could he mask his rage and panic. With a false smile he asked, ''They attacked, therefore they know. But *how*—if there has been no compromise? How did they know?''

''The Nicaraguans say there are many attacks on the coast. The fascists kill Cubans and Soviets and Sandinista leaders. It was only bad luck for your men. If the fascists knew of your mission, they would have taken Choufi and Gabriel as prisoners, not killed them.''

Dastgerdi nodded. ''True. ''

A public-address voice announced the departure of the flight to Syria. Dastgerdi rose, discreetly waved to the informant and disappeared into a crowd of embarking passengers.

Despite their precautions and belief that they had not been noticed, the meeting of Dastgerdi and his informant had indeed been studied with interest. Across the lounge, a French counterintelligence agent noted the number and destination of Dastgerdi's flight and continued to watch his unidentified contact.

As Dastgerdi flew to Damascus, the French counterintelligence office transmitted his information to an Agency contact in the United States.

4

Rock and roll blared from the television. Dancers kicked and spun as a singer postured. Colored images exploded through galactic space.

Sprawled on the hotel bed, Gadgets Schwarz drained another can of beer, aimed the empty at Carl Lyons's head and threw. The can hit its target, bounced off, then disappeared out the window. Lyons leaned over the railing to watch it fall through the canyon between the high rises.

Lyons dodged as Gadgets opened another beer and motioned to throw it through the window.

"Don't! You'll kill someone down there!"

"Never!" Gadgets gulped the beer, belched and continued, foam spilling down face and neck. "I'll never throw away a full beer!"

He took a final slug, and tossed the empty. Lyons caught it in midair. He crushed it in his fist and sighted on his partner's face.

Gadgets dived from the bed. The nightstand fell. The lamp crashed. Lyons held his throw and maneuvered for an unobstructed line of fire.

Dodging around the bed, he prepared to throw. A blast of beer foam sprayed him. Gadgets jumped up, shaking a beer can and jetting foam. Holding another can in his left hand, he lifted the pop-top with his teeth. A can in each hand, he drove Lyons from the room.

"And don't come back without your own six-pack!"

After Lyons threw it, the crumpled can ricochetted off the closing door. He heard Gadgets shriek as the can scored. "Got him!"

"Deescalate, jokers," Blancanales said from a doorway across the corridor. "You'll have the police up here."

Wiping beer from his face and sport shirt, Lyons crossed to Blancanales. "He's having a one-man party in there. Any news from D.C.?"

"The interrogation's continuing." Blancanales looked up and down the corridor, saw no one. "Go ahead, take the day off. Get a six-pack. Get six six-packs. They'll call when they know where we're going."

"Lebanon?"

"Wherever that Iranian went."

"Yeah, wherever that is. Later."

Lyons returned to his room as the phone rang. The desk clerk told him: "A Mr. Randall and a Mr. Lloyd are here. Shall I send them up?"

Lyons recalled the two men from a manufacturing shop in Baltimore—an Agency shop for the manufacture and maintenance of special weapons. "Put Randall on the phone."

A moment later a voice came over the receiver. "Hey, man. You're living in style here."

"All day. Maybe tonight. Then we're gone."

"Yeah, I know. I got some going-away presents for you."

"The Company send them?"

Randall heard the suspicion in Carl Lyons's voice. "Lloyd and me only work *for* them, you know? We used to work *with* Andrzej. There's a difference. You know what I mean?"

"Come on up. You want drinks, food? Tell the desk to send up whatever you want."

"There in a flash."

Lyons keyed the numbers for his partners' rooms, told them some Company guys were coming up to visit, and to listen for any problems.

A knock sounded within minutes. Lyons took his Colt Python from his suitcase, set it on the dresser and covered it with a shirt. Then he opened the door.

Randall was a wiry, conservatively dressed, middle-aged black with short hair and a mischievous smile. In both hands he carried a large, plainly wrapped box. Behind him, a beer-bellied Anglo with thinning blond hair stood with a long, flat box under his arm. Unlike Randall, Lloyd wore work clothes—boots, jeans, plaid shirt, denim jacket.

"Glad we caught you before you left," Randall told Lyons, handing over the box. "Here's your surprise."

Lyons almost dropped it. "What is this? Feels like—"

"Kalashnikov mags. With a total of three hundred rounds of 7.62mm ComBloc ammunition. Hand-loaded with absolutely exact charges and hollowpoints for accuracy and impact that you got to see to believe."

"Hollowpoints?"

"Wipeouts," Lloyd said.

"Wish you had time to come down to the shop." Randall opened the box, removed one of the curving magazines, thumbed out a cartridge. Holding up the stubby ComBloc round, he pointed to the bullet. "You fire this little thing into a ten-pound block of wet clay—which happens to have a mass and texture remarkably similar to meat—and you got ten pounds of clay everywhere but where it was."

"But I don't use an AK," Lyons told them.

"You will where you're going," Randall countered.

"Where's that?"

Randall looked at Lloyd; they laughed.

"Really, I don't know. Do you?"

"If you don't," said Lloyd, "we can't tell you. Maybe you don't have clearance. Company policy. But here's something for when you get there."

He opened the long box to reveal a battered, scuffed Kalashnikov.

Lifting it, Randall pulled out the magazine and jerked back the cocking handle several times. "Looks like shit," he said. "But it's special. Check it out."

Pulling back the cocking handle once more to confirm the empty chamber, Lyons touched the trigger. It snapped without the usual long travel. He tried the other mechanisms. The safety-selector lever moved without the standard "AK clack." The magazine release had no sharp edges. The rear tangent sight had been delicately filed to a perfect fit. The meter scale had been touched up with white. A second flip-up sight with two small white dots had been added. Lyons cupped his hand over the sight and saw the glow of tritium dots. He examined the front sight. The protective ring had been cut to wings to allow faster aiming. A small flip-up sight completed the night-sight modification.

"Like a Galil...."

"You got it."

Lyons closed and opened the folding steel stock. It locked and unlocked without wobbling. He cocked the rifle again, sighted on a distant roof, squeezed off an imaginary shot at a pigeon. "Perfect." He tried the rifle in his hands, jerking it repeatedly to his shoulder. It felt right. He closed the steel stock and studied it.

"It's longer—it's the right size," Lyons raved. "Where'd you get this?"

"We made it," Randall answered. "Feel how it's heavier? That's 'cause we used good steel. And, man, it shoots fine. Superfine. At a hundred yards, most AKs can't quite keep a group in the black. This one shoots two-inch groups, even with the folding stock. How's that?"

Lyons phoned his partners. "Want to meet some friends of Konzaki's?"

They arrived at the same time as the room service cart. Blocking the view of the bellboy, Blancanales wheeled in the ice and beer and sandwiches. Gadgets tipped the bellboy with a handful of foreign coins and an American dollar.

In the room, they popped beers while Lyons made introductions.. The American-made Kalashnikov became the center of conversation. But the talk soon turned to Able Team's assignment.

"We can't tell you," Randall said, laughing. "I mean, if you don't know—"

"Lebanon?" Blancanales asked.

"I thought you didn't know," Randall responded.

"What is this game?" Lyons demanded. "On the plane, back home, over the phone, no one makes any sense. We had this clerk jerk briefing us, and he wouldn't give us straight answers. What goes on? I have to know—"

Lloyd answered. "The Agency is strange. If you understand that, you're on your way to understanding the problem."

"Yeah, yeah. I know all about it, but—"

"Then why are you asking?" Randall countered.

The phone interrupted the joking. Lyons took the call, listened for a good many seconds without saying a word before hanging up. "We're on our way."

"Where?" Gadgets and Blancanales asked in unison.

Lyons grinned. "Can't tell you."

"THE BEKAA...." Now it was Grimaldi who operated the slide projector. He punched a button and an aerial photograph of a village appeared on the screen.

Taken by a low-orbit spy satellite, the picture showed an abandoned village surrounded by rocky, untended fields. A road wound through foothills to the outermost of a series of concentric perimeters. An open area between the first and second perimeters had evenly spaced depressions in the soil—mines. Guardhouses set at intervals along the second perimeter provided interlocking fields of fire. A band of bare soil separated the second perimeter from the innermost. Grimaldi glanced to his briefing papers, then pointed to each ring of wire and machine-gun emplacements.

"This one is razor wire eight feet high. This is a minefield—and that's for sure. Look at this." He pointed to what appeared to be a large crater where one mine had exploded. "The second perimeter is chain link and razor wire. These are sandbagged bunkers and towers overlooking the minefield. And they've got guard dogs between the guard positions and the last perimeter, which is a stone wall topped with razor wire and broken glass set in—"

Lyons interrupted. "How can they be positive about the dogs?"

"Where's the superzoom?" Grimaldi fumbled with the controls, finally hit a lever. "Look for yourself." The image expanded, the outer perimeters going off-screen, the mosaic of rooftops becoming blocks of gray and black, the head and arms of a sentry appearing on the top of the wall. Grimaldi pointed to a form on the earth: a dog.

"That's positive," Lyons agreed.

"Your folders have prints of all this," Grimaldi continued. "We've done everything conceivable to make your infiltration possible—"

"Infiltration?" Gadgets asked, amazed. "You think we're supermen?"

"Or invisible?" Lyons asked.

"Or expendable?" Blancanales asked.

"Expendable invisible men, we ain't," Gadgets emphasized. "No way."

"There isn't any other way," Grimaldi told them.

He pressed the button, flipping back to the slide showing the position of the base. "Here's the village. Only a few kilometers from the Syrian border. Here... here...and here—missile sites. The Israeli air force can't knock out the missiles because the sites are crewed by Soviets. And there's hundreds of antiaircraft positions along the Marjayoun-Baalbek highway. So we can't have the Israelis send in planes and bomb it."

"We'll be going in by helicopter?" Blancanales asked.

"No, you'll be in cars."

Lyons groaned.

"Listen!" Grimaldi pointed to the mountains east of Beirut. "Contract agents will transport you from the coast. The Agency prepared all the identity documents you'll need to get through the checkpoints outside Beirut. Then you'll only have to worry about checkpoints along the highway. All these villages along here are controlled by the Islamic Amal and the Iranians and Libyans—"

"Hey, Ironman," Gadgets turned abruptly to Lyons. "Think I could pass as an Iranian?"

"No."

"Neither can you."

"When you get to the village nearest the base," Grimaldi continued, "then you march cross-country."

Blancanales shook his head. "When we get there? *If* we get there."

"That's the plan?" Lyons asked, incredulous. "We make like tourists and drive in, then hike to the base and blow it away? That's the plan the Agency took weeks to create?"

"Not quite—there's more." Grimaldi read from a memo. "'The team must make penetration of objective. Disposition of threat will remain uncertain without team observation of weapons, organization and sponsorship prior to termination of threat.'"

"Oh...." Lyons nodded. "We take notes, too. Maybe we can get an interview with the Number One Ayatollah. Wizard, did you bring your camera?"

"See what happens when you mouth off at Agency clerks?" Gadgets asked Lyons. "They bring us jive missions like this. Wish that George dude was here now. Send him on this insane joyride."

Lyons looked at his partners. He signaled a thumbs-down opinion of the Agency plan. But then he said, "Tell them we didn't like it, but we'll do it. We'll do the best we can. Follow our instructions to the letter. Do or die. Stiff upper lip. Hip, hip."

Blancanales spoke next. "Any last-minute developments on Dastgerdi?"

"French security people confirmed that Dastgerdi passed through Paris on his return to the Middle East. Oh, yeah. Here's another detail the Agency people want you to watch for. Dastgerdi's coordinating this project, keeping the Iranians and Syrians together. And the Soviets, the Agency assumes. But there's one more thing they want you to watch for. It seems a courier passed information to Dastgerdi in a passenger lounge in the Paris airport. But listen to this: the courier didn't come from the Soviet Union. The courier came from and returned to Baghdad, the capital of Iraq."

"What do the Iraqis have to do with this?" Blancanales asked. "They're at war with the Iranians. The Iraqis wouldn't work with the Iranians."

"It's a mystery," Grimaldi agreed. "Maybe it'll make your trip more interesting."

"Yeah—" Lyons laughed bitterly "—interesting."

5

As the three members of Able Team stepped from the warmth of the hired van, a gust of wind hit them with freezing sleet. The driver gunned the engine impatiently as the Americans unloaded their trunks. Without a word, he reversed the van and drove away into the night.

Gadgets looked around at the shacks lining the muddy road. Even in the storm, the air stank of diesel and rotting fish. "Ain't Club Med."

Gripping his two heavy trunks of gear, Lyons staggered to the dock. An old coastal cruiser lurched in the storm chop, the dock creaking as the cruiser pulled the heavy mooring lines taut with every sway. A crewman in a yellow rain slicker saw him and waved a flashlight.

Voices shouted in Greek. Silhouettes moved across lighted ports. Lyons stopped at the head of the gangplank and put down his trunks. As he waited for his partners, his eyes scanned the cruiser.

On the deck, plastic tarps covered stacks of cargo. A hoist arm overhung the crates, its steel cables banging with every gust. Light came from two levels of cabins. Lyons saw men inside the lighted pilothouse. His eyes searched for anything—any detail, any motion—that meant a trap.

After landing in Nicosia, Cyprus, they had called Lebanon and spoken with Captain Powell, the Marine on detached duty with the Shia militias of West Beirut. They did not risk briefing him on their mission to the Bekaa over the phone, saying only that they would be "taking a drive together." A few weeks before, Powell had accompanied Able Team to Mexico as they pursued and exterminated a terror force of Iranian Revolutionary Guards. He would know why they called.

"Thought they had a hovercraft to Beirut," Gadgets commented. "Don't know if I want to go out in a storm in that bucket."

"The boat," Blancanales emphasized, "is not our number-one worry."

"Let's go." Lyons took his trunks. "If these guys try to take us, we'll take the boat."

In a car parked between two shacks across the road, Anne Desmarais watched Able Team board the cruiser.

Though the young woman's visa documents listed her occupation as a Canadian journalist based in Quebec, she served the KGB as agent and courier. Her role exploited her credentials as a Canadian journalist to travel freely throughout Central America, carrying messages for Stalinist guerrillas and gathering information for her Soviet masters. These KGB-financed travels also provided the background for her articles denouncing the imperialism and aggression of the United States, while their sale to Canadian and European newspapers provided a legitimate source of income to explain the thousands of U.S. dollars she received from the Soviets.

Desmarais had already encountered and identified

Able Team through Captain Powell, the Marine officer working for the CIA in Beirut.

On a West Beirut boulevard a month before, a terrorist group had ambushed and annihilated a CIA unit investigating a meeting between Iranian Revolutionary Guards and a Libyan diplomat. Powell, a member of the ambushed unit, had survived only by luck. But his superiors in Washington did not accept that explanation. Powell had developed a close camaraderie with the Shia militias fighting for the reform of the Lebanese government. His superiors, suspicious of all non-Christian and non-Israeli contacts, assumed that Powell's loyalty had been bought by Syrian gold. He received a blunt order to return to Washington for debriefing. Powell knew his career with the Central Intelligence Agency had ended—unless he could prove himself innocent. He had to find the assassins. . . .

Playing the role of an investigative journalist, Desmarais had approached Powell with the offer of a meeting with a member of the assassination squad, Oshakkar, an American Black Muslim fighting with the fanatics of the Islamic Amal gang. Oshakkar, a proponent of a heretical Islamic sect founded on racial hatred and the demand for a "New Africa" in the American South, wanted out of the gang and would trade information for dollars and a ticket to the United States.

Desmarais supported her story about Oshakkar with photos of the ambush taken from the point of view of the killers. The photos proved she had witnessed the slaughter of the CIA unit. She also had photos of the Iranian and Syrian leaders of the terrorist group. Powell agreed to meet with Oshakkar.

It was a trap. Iranian Revolutionary Guards kidnapped Desmarais. The gang of Iranians clubbed Powell unconscious with their Kalashnikov rifles, and he would have been captured had not Carl Lyons and his Konzak selective-fire assault shotgun intervened. Later, Powell had led a combined force of Able Team and Shia militiamen through the sewers and ruins of Beirut to rescue Desmarais.

Though beaten and raped by the Iranians, Desmarais said she wanted to continue "on the story." She told Powell and Able Team she had overheard a conversation in Spanish between a Libyan and a Nicaraguan in which they mentioned a meeting place in Mexico. Offering this information, she persuaded Powell to allow her to accompany him and Able Team to Mexico.

In Mexico City, a KGB squad alerted by Desmarais seized her and Powell and Blancanales. But Gadgets Schwarz had planted a miniature transmitter on Desmarais. Monitoring the transmission, Gadgets heard and recorded a conversation between Desmarais and Cultural Attaché Illovich of the Soviet embassy as they plotted the deaths of Powell and Able Team.

With the assistance of an elite antiterrorist force of the Mexican army, Able Team captured Desmarais and Illovich. However, a Mexican officer refused to allow any executions. Able Team compromised by forcing Illovich to cooperate in the pursuit. Then, to prevent the Soviet and Canadian from betraying the Americans to the terrorists, Able Team transported the prisoners north into the Mexican deserts. There they allowed Illovich and Desmarais to escape.

Desmarais became one of the few Soviet agents to encounter Able Team and survive. Now, in Cyprus, she proved her value to the KGB. She flipped on a radio transmitter and reported in French, "Yankee travelers confirmed. Repeat, Yankee travelers confirmed. They depart on their voyage. Please arrange for transfer."

A voice answered. "Received. Transfer dispatched."

Switching off the radio, Desmarais watched with satisfaction as the cruiser moved away from the dock. The Americans would never reach Lebanon.

Two hundred kilometers of the Mediterranean Sea separate Cyprus from Lebanon. Somewhere in that stretch, their voyage would end.

LYONS SAW THE FLASHING LIGHT. Standing alone in the storm, a plastic tarp draped over him, he saw the light flash in repeating sequences of dots and dashes. The distant boat broke through the ocean swells, the light appearing in the darkness, then disappearing as the boat carrying Lyons dropped into a trough.

Though he could not decipher it, he recognized the flashing as a code. He turned to the steamed windows of the passenger cabin, saw the blurry forms of his partners. Blancanales and Gadgets had their shipping trunks open. He saw the vague outlines of Blancanales's M-16/M-203 disassembled on the white sheet of the bed. Gadgets was leaning over his trunk, organizing weapons and gear.

Lyons opened the door and leaned inside. "There's a ship signaling."

"What are the Greeks doing?" Blancanales asked. His hands moved in a blur, reassembling his weapon.

"I'll check."

Outside again, he heard voices coming from the pilothouse. Lyons looked up and saw shadows moving on the fogged windows. Reaching under his coat, he checked his modified-for-silence Colt Government Model. The awkward pistol rode under his left arm in a customized shoulder holster. In the small of his back, he wore his standard Colt Python, loaded with X-head hollowpoints.

Half-hidden by the cargo tarp, Lyons crept up the companionway to the pilothouse. The swaying and bucking of the cruiser as it broke through the swells threw him against the steel wall. But his shoulder striking the ship made only one more creak in the cacophony of rattling and shuddering and crashing sounds. Lyons moved slowly to the top of the companionway, then pressed his back against the pilothouse.

The Greeks were speaking. One voice originated in the pilothouse, another from a radio. The radio voice issued commands. The other argued and cursed, but finally went quiet. In the darkness of the ocean, Lyons saw that the distant light no longer flashed.

He heard the Greek crew talking inside the pilothouse. Then someone crossed the floor and the door banged open.

Two men in raincoats hurried down the companionway, one carrying a pistol, the other a shotgun sawed off to a pistol grip with eighteen inches of barrel.

Lyons's hand went to the pocket radio in his coat.

He pressed the transmit key in a rapid series of clicks: the team code for alert.

Below him, the Greek with the pistol entered the cabin. The man with the shotgun followed. Lyons waited. He heard nothing—no shots, no fighting, nothing. Finally, his hand-radio buzzed.

"What goes with these bozos?" Gadgets jived. "Don't they know to knock? Rude dudes!"

"You got them?"

Blancanales answered. "The one that speaks English says a ship is threatening them. They're to hand us over or get sunk. Is it coming?"

"Yeah, I see it out there. I'm going up top. I'll take it over. Come up when you can."

"Got it."

Dropping his black plastic camouflage, Lyons slipped out his silenced Colt and snapped back the slide to chamber the first hollowpoint of the extended 10-round magazine. Then he swung down the left-hand grip lever. Throwing the door open, he grasped the selective-fire Colt with both hands and stepped inside.

A crewman at the wheel stared at the American without moving. The Greek at the radio made his final mistake in reaching for the tiny automatic on the table.

Three .45-caliber hollowpoints smashed through his chest and throat, a mist of blood spraying from his mouth. He fell back against the shelves of maps and technical manuals, his hands rising toward his wounds but never touching the blood-spurting holes. Dead, he fell forward, his legs kicking in a last spasm.

Stepping to the radio table, Lyons took the 9mm pistol and pocketed it. The other Greek kept his hands on the wheel, but stared, fascinated and sickened by the sudden death of the radioman.

A voice came from the radio in Greek, barking short commands. Lyons didn't touch the radio. The voice continued, rising to a shout.

As the white brilliance of a searchlight swept the cruiser, Blancanales rushed into the pilothouse with the M-16/M-203 and the American-made Kalashnikov. A bandolier of 5.56mm mags and 40mm grenades crossed his chest.

"Take all this." Blancanales passed the Kalashnikov and a handful of ComBloc mags to Lyons. "I'm going to try to bluff them off."

Glass exploded. Wind and freezing rain filled the interior of the pilothouse, then the machine gun on the other craft flashed again. A tracer streaked through one shattered window and out another.

Lyons snapped back the cocking handle of the Kalashnikov. "Forget the talk, Pol. Put a grenade into that."

Rounds from Gadgets's CAR assault rifle pinged off the searchlight, shattering the lens. The light flashed and dimmed to black. The machine gun, either a U.S. .50-caliber or a Soviet 12.7mm weapon, answered with a burst. The cruiser shuddered with the impacts, the heavy slugs tearing through steel like paper. Lyons motioned for the Greek on the floor to stay there. Then he flipped up the night sights of the Kalashnikov, aimed and fired.

He could not see where the slugs hit. Fighting the lurching of the cruiser, he held the three tritium glowing dots on line with the flashing muzzle of the attacker's weapon. A ricochet sparked from the pedestal-mounted weapon. Lyons snapped off a series of 2- and 3-shot bursts. Then the heavy weapon of his attacker whipped upward, dying hands firing a long, wild burst into the sky.

Blancanales fired across the thirty meters of water to the faint lights of the other craft's wheelhouse. The searing chemical flame of white phosphorous sprayed the side of the shadowy craft, burning away the darkness, revealing a motor yacht. Wood and plastic flamed.

"Hit them again!" Lyons shouted. He sighted above the fire. His bursts of ComBloc-caliber hollowpoints raked the windows of the yacht.

Autorifle muzzles flashed as gunmen returned the fire. Slugs hammered the steel cruiser, ricochets zinging through the pilothouse. Blancanales fired again and white light illuminated the interior of the yacht. Lyons sighted on a silhouette and fired a burst.

Against the white fire, the twisted silhouette became a man with an arm bending at a new joint, then a casualty as he fell into the ocean. The yacht veered away, white light and flames visible through the back windows. A form climbed a ladder to the top, where the machine gun spun on its mount. Lyons and Gadgets fired simultaneously, the storm-sway throwing off their aim. The climber finally fell backward to the rear deck.

Blancanales fired again and scored with high explosive. Shrapnel ripped the interior of the wheelhouse, killing or wounding everyone inside. The yacht pitched and heaved as it circled, the controls jammed in a right turn. Flames leaped from the shattered windows, the wind whipping away black smoke.

"We'll get the survivors. . . ." Blancanales motioned for the Greek helmsman to slow the cruiser and turn back.

On the yacht, two men struggled with an inflated raft. Lyons sighted on them, lining up the three tritium dots, and fired. One man fell, the other staggered backward off the yacht. The wind threw the torn and deflated raft into the water.

"What survivors?" Lyons asked.

Able Team's cruiser continued eastward, leaving the flaming hulk behind.

6

As the eastern horizon grayed with the first minutes of day, the coastal cruiser eased up to a jetty and bumped to a stop against a pier of timbers and old tires. Workers left a fire and extended a long gangplank to the deck. The surviving Greek crewmen secured the gangplank as the first man wheeled aboard a pushcart.

Lyons saw trucks on the beach. Militiamen with rifles slung over their backs crowded around another fire. Beyond the beach, Lyons saw only gray, snow-splotched hills.

Blancanales spoke quietly to one of the Greeks. "There'll be no problems if you just let us walk away."

"No problems, no more problems. We have enough problems." The Greek looked at the machine-gunned pilothouse. Along one side of the cruiser, innumerable slugs of various calibers had punched through the steel bulkheads and doors. Seeing a laborer with a pushcart, the Greek jerked up one of Able Team's heavy trunks.

"Here. Take to beach. Hurry."

The Greek pointed to the other trunks and suitcases, then the pushcart. The worker—dressed in thick winter clothes with a heavy wool cap pulled down low on his face so that only his beard and eyes showed—

put the trunk on the pushcart, grunting with the labor. But when the Greek crewman walked away, the worker looked up at Lyons.

"What you got in here, specialist?" The worker asked. "Dirty tricks?"

Lyons recognized the voice. "Powell!"

"Hey, it's the Marine," Gadgets said, his voice low. "Looks like tough times since you quit the Agency."

"I'm back on the payroll. But I ain't here to lift weights. Get your stuff on the cart so we can move. Looks like something happened to this boat."

"We'll tell you when we're out of here."

They muscled the pushcart up the plank. As they wove through the stream of workers unloading the cargo, Powell kept his face down. Lyons waited until they neared the trucks before explaining.

"We got intercepted. They told the crew to hand us over. We took the boat and wasted the other one."

"Any idea who it was?"

"Maybe Soviets. Probably Agency. Only the Agency knew we'd be on the boat."

"Any prisoners left to question?"

Lyons laughed quickly and cynically. "Any more jokes? Let's talk business. We called you because we're ditching our Agency connections. We're on our way into the Bekaa—"

Now Powell laughed. "Hey, crazy guy. I'm your contact man."

"What! Why didn't they tell us that?"

"Washington called weeks ago and told me to start prepping for a shot into the Bekaa. But they wouldn't say with who or when. Knew it had to be something to do with the *E*-ranies we wasted in Mexico and I asked about you all, but the Agency kept saying it was Need to Know Only. They finally called me yesterday and told me a team would be coming in. But until you called from Nicosia, I didn't know it would be you.''

"Those clerks..." Lyons sneered.

"If I'd known it was the Three Cowboys of the Apocalypse, I could've mounted a real production. Let's get your gear into the truck.''

Powell threw open the doors to a panel van. "But the real problem is the Syrian situation. I don't know if we'll be able to get into the Bekaa now. We should've done this a week ago. Now, I don't know...."

"Syria?" Blancanales asked as he lifted cases. "What now?"

"Something's gone wrong with Hafez Assad, the president of Syria. He was scheduled to appear in Damascus and he didn't. Maybe he had another heart attack. Maybe he died. Army units loyal to him circled the city and took positions on the highways. This isn't for sure, but there are reports of his troops fighting with the Defense Forces, which are the troops of his brother, who figures he's next in line to be president.''

"What is it? A royal family?" Lyons asked. He got into the van and sat on a trunk. "One prince fighting another for the throne?''

"Not royalty, just a gang of warlords.''

"What's the difference?" Lyons snapped back.

"A few hundred years. Maybe Hafez is dead, maybe not," Powell said, helping Gadgets. "The fighting's going on but it might not be Hafez Assad against

Rifaat Assad. That's the problem. If it's not the Assads fighting, who is it? Might be Ali Haidar, the brother-in-law of Rifaat. Maybe he's decided to be president.''

''A brother-in-law?'' Lyons shook his head at the politics. ''What about the sister? Maybe she wants to be the queen?''

''Who knows what she wants? It could be the Muslim Brotherhood again. Or maybe the Shias or—''

Blancanales interrupted. ''How does all this affect the mission?''

His hands on the truck's doors, Powell stopped. He looked to the east. ''Listen. . . .''

ON THE HIGHWAY, over the sound of tires on the wet asphalt, they heard artillery. Powell leaned forward to Hussein and spoke in Arabic. The Lebanese driver passed him a battery-powered AM radio. Powell spun through the dial, listening to snatches of Arabic and French and English. Some stations programmed rock and roll, others the music of traditional Islamic society. Powell listened to one announcer intone a solemn monologue in Arabic.

After a minute, Gadgets asked, ''So what's he saying?''

''Another storm's coming. More snow.''

''What about Syria?'' Lyons asked.

''This radio can't bring in the Damascus stations. When we get to Akbar's, I'll listen in on what's coming out of Syria. That'll be interesting.''

''I thought Syria was a controlled society,'' Blancanales commented. ''If there were a coup in progress, would the regime allow news broadcasts?''

Powell laughed. "Who's talking about news? It's the jive line that I got to hear. Or the absence of jive. The music changes for a coup. If Hafez is dead, it'll either be upper music or downer music. If it's a serious coup, there'll be patriotic songs, military marches. If it's a *very* serious coup, you might hear shooting on the radio. Heard that one time. Deejay's rapping right along, playing pop rock and bebopping, then it's a shootout in Studio RKO."

The political speculation helped pass the time in the back of the closed van. The travelers heard traffic noise and distant shellfire outside. After an hour and three stops at checkpoints, the van descended a steep ramp and a steel door clanked shut behind it.

Opening the doors, they stepped into an underground parking garage. Bare lights ten meters above their heads illuminated stacks of open shipping crates.

Thousands of automatic rifles, squad automatic weapons, heavy machine guns, rocket launchers, grenade launchers and mortars filled the stacked crates. Tons of ammunition—in original boxes and boxes that once held cooking oil or detergent or stereo components—were piled nearby.

"Superior firepower," Lyons commented.

"There's a war right there," Gadgets added.

"You got it," Powell told them. "That's Amal weapons. The government's organizing a national reconciliation, so Amal retired all the second-string boys."

"Second string?" Gadgets asked. "You mean there's more out there?"

"Yeah, the trusted units, the ones directly under the

command of the Shia leadership—the ones that take orders and maintain discipline—are still out there, loaded and locked. Waiting for the government to break down or fuck up or the Syrians to invade.''

"Amal, huh?" Lyons's eyes narrowed. "We're going to the Bekaa to waste an Amal camp. We ought to start with a demo job here.''

Powell shook his head. "You got to get the names straight. Could lead to real serious difficulties. This is Amal. They're okay. I work with them. They broke the fascist Maronites and forced the government to start counting the Shias as people. It's *Islamic* Amal out in the Bekaa. They're the ones working with the Iranians. Amal fights the Islamic Amal all the time, along with the Iranians and the Libyans and Palestinians. Sometimes Syrians, too.''

"How do you keep the politics straight?" Blancanales asked.

"You don't!" Powell laughed. "You can't! It's insane.'' He reached into the van, removed his short-barreled Galil and slung it over his shoulder. "The rule is, They Shoot, You Shoot. Simple, easy to remember. Let's go look at the transportation we're making for your tour of the beautiful Bekaa Valley, heartland of Lebanon.''

The Marine captain led Able Team along the wall of weapons and munitions. The racks of weapons continued the length of the garage. The end of the garage had been knocked out with jackhammers or explosives to connect with the garage of the next building. There, men worked on vehicles: a Land Rover, a Mercedes troop truck, and semitrucks and trailer.

Militiamen with wrenches and welding torches looked up at the four Americans. Powell rushed over to them, shaking hands, embracing them, looking at the work. Able Team waited three steps away.

Blancanales studied the Marine. Powell wore dirty slacks and an old sweater. His shaggy hair covered his ears and collar, merging with his beard. Though his skin and hair color did not quite match the tones of the Lebanese, he looked like one of them, standing there in the group, talking in Arabic and joking, the militiamen pointing to the vehicles and answering the American's questions.

Now he understood why the Agency had doubted Powell's loyalty. Captain Powell, USMC, had gone native. Some point after months of friendships and shared dangers, after days of working in street Arabic and then making formal reports in bureaucratic English, Powell had ceased to be an American officer working liaison with foreign militias and had become a soldier among friends. He had continued typing reports and answering questions and making evaluations of political shifts in the Shia militias, but his superiors had noted the shift in perspective. No longer did he stand outside, observing and reporting. After the change, he stood inside and attempted to explain.

In Southeast Asia, Blancanales had seen Green Berets go native. Month after month, soldiers had lived in remote hamlets without seeing any Americans but the Green Berets in their small units. They lived with Montagnards or Cambodians or Laotians, eating their food, caring for their children, fighting their enemies. Only radios had maintained the link to the

American command. When uniforms rotted or wore out, the Americans wore the traditional handmade clothing of the people. When the last of their rations was gone, the Americans turned to local foods. Finally months of loneliness and isolation and the flirting of village girls made them overcome the official prohibition, and they took local women.

Once Blancanales had marched to a hamlet with a squad of men and a mission to execute. Looking for the U.S. Special Forces sergeant in charge of the tribal militia, he had been approached by a man taller and heavier than the others. Under the Montagnard clothing and sandals, the PAVN web gear, the sun-darkened skin, Blancanales somehow recognized the sergeant. He had briefed the sergeant on the objective, and the sergeant had conferred with the village men. Squatting, the sergeant scratched a map and two trails in the dirt, saying, "We'll go this way and you'll take the other trail." When the sergeant said "we," he meant himself and the Montagnards, not himself and Blancanales's squad of Americans.

The transformation of Captain Powell from CIA liaison officer to American with the Shias had alarmed his officers in the Agency. They doubted his loyalty. And Blancanales understood why. Powell's superiors in the Agency were graduates of the conservative Ivy League universities, men prejudiced by generation after generation of wealth and privilege, who often stepped from the conference rooms of the Agency to the boardrooms of multinational corporations. They could never understand why an American of a God-fearing Texas heritage, a commissioned officer in the

United States Marine Corps, would accept the customs and politics of an oppressed non-Christian people in a war-ravaged nation.

Calling to Able Team, Powell broke Blancanales's line of thought and confirmed his conclusions. Powell motioned them into the circle of Shia militiamen mechanics.

"Hey, meet my friends. You know Akbar—he went to Mexico with us. And this is...."

After making introductions, Powell guided the Americans away. "We're not finished yet on the transportation, so I'm taking you for a meal and some sleep, if you want it. We'll all be going in tonight; it's all arranged, so don't you all even think about it. I know how you cowboys operate and it'll be ready. We got it all under control."

When Powell said "we," Blancanales knew the Marine did not mean "we Americans." Blancanales understood.

7

Anne Desmarais rode through the streets of Beirut in a taxi. She listened to a radio announcer reporting the continuing progress of the new coalition to restore peace in Lebanon. The station cut to a telephone interview with a spokesman in Damascus who assured the public that the decrees had the full support of Syria.

Desmarais looked for the changes. At checkpoints, her eyes scanned the faces and uniforms of the soldiers. The new government coalition had moved to restore the authority of the Lebanese army by replacing the Falangist militias with Christians in army uniforms. Shia militiamen, shaved, their hair trimmed to official length, now wore army uniforms.

In the ruined no-man's-land that had been the Green Line, the piles of sand and rock blocking boulevards had been removed. The people walked around the tangles of wire and mines that divided their neighborhoods.

In West Beirut, schools and shops had reopened. Many merchants still operated behind walls of sandbags, but others had replaced the glass in their windows so that shoppers could see displays. Repairmen worked on streetlights and telephone lines without fear of snipers.

A victory for world socialism, the young Canadian woman thought. Defeat the American dogs of imperialism and peace comes. Only after the Lebanese drove out the Americans and embraced their Soviet and Syrian brothers in world revolution did social harmony return to this ancient land.

Now only the Zionists remained to be defeated, Desmarais thought. If the united Arab peoples drove the Jews out of south Lebanon, then continued in their relentless jihad of holy revenge and destroyed the cursed Zionist entity and restored the Palestinians to their rightful homes—

"Listen to this!" Interrupting her daydreaming, the taxi driver turned up the radio. "Those Syrians are making war on themselves. As if there has not been enough killing. Heaven help us all if those animals—"

"It is the Americans or the Israelis," she told him in her Quebecois French. "They started it somehow...."

"What did you say? The Americans? The Israelis? Impossible! How could they be involved? Those Syrians need no foreigners to kill one another. They will do it for any reason, they—"

"I paid you to drive! Not lecture. I know the truth. Now, drive!"

"Yes, *mademoiselle*. Of course."

They rode in silence to the street where Sayed Ahamed maintained the headquarters of his militia forces in a shell-shattered hotel. Despite the "normalization," concrete barriers still blocked both ends. The thick concrete cubes forced vehicles to snake through several tight turns to approach the hotel. Positions with machine guns and rocket launchers surveyed the street. And without exception, no vehicles were permitted to park on the street. There would be no car bombs here.

Stopping at the first militia checkpoint, the driver turned off the engine and handed a teenage soldier the key to the trunk. Other militiamen searched the interior of the taxi and slid mirrors underneath to check for explosives.

An officer questioned the driver, then Desmarais. "He says you are a journalist. Present your credentials."

She handed him her passport and a government form listing her news syndicate, her nationality, blood type and next of kin. The officer examined the signatures and seals of the documents, then stepped into a sandbag bunker. While he telephoned his commander, the militiamen completed their search by looking under the car seats.

One of the teenagers put a hand under her coat and frisked her for weapons. She slapped him away and all the other militiamen laughed.

The officer returned. "Commander Ahamed tells you to hurry. Urgent business."

Shells exploded in the mountains east of the city. The soldiers walked to the shelter of sandbags. The street cleared of pedestrians.

As the officer returned her papers, he cursed. "Unholy Syrian dogs, eating Communist shit, copulating with the Soviets—go, woman! Get to safety! The dying starts again soon."

The driver gunned the engine and whipped through

the course of concrete cubes. He sped to the doors of the hotel. "Out! Move! I have a family. I cannot wait!"

"But I paid for the trip back to my hotel!"

"Here! Take the money!" The driver threw a handful of bills at her.

Desmarais collected the crumpled money from the seat. The driver ran around the taxi and dragged her out. She screamed and slapped him; he pushed her to the sidewalk and sped away.

As the shells crashed in the mountains, Desmarais counted the Lebanese pounds. The taxi driver had shortchanged her! Even as he had panicked, he had made a few pounds, returning not half the money but only an approximate sum.

"You cheated me, you bastard!" she shouted at the retreating taxi.

Inside the hotel, guards searched her politely and professionally. They waved metal detectors over her body. They checked her camera kit, the lens of her camera, the batteries in her cassette recorder.

A militiaman picked up a telephone and keyed a number. He announced Desmarais, giving her physical description and document numbers.

Very thorough, she noted. She would include the information in her next report.

"Come with me, please," a young militia officer requested in perfect French. They stopped at an elevator door.

"Does it actually operate?" Desmarais asked.

"Certainly. What interesting French you speak! You cannot be from Africa?"

"No!" she snapped. "Quebec!"

"Oh, the state in America."

"No, Canada." She studied his face. "You are very young to be an officer. Are you a hero?"

"Oh, no. But I am very . . . exacting. I studied to be a doctor. My commander recognized my abilities and assigned me to this post. I must be an officer to instruct the soldiers, so I am an officer. It is only a matter of convenience."

"But soon you will return to your studies. You must be glad."

"How can I return? The war, you understand."

"But the war is over. The Council has unified the city and reorganized the army—"

"There can be no peace while the Syrian dogs and their masters occupy our country."

"The Syrians are friends of Lebanon. They came only to help and rebuild what the Zionists and CIA—"

The young man cut her off with laughter. The elevator opened, and he escorted her past militiamen with automatic rifles to a suite crowded with typewriters and files.

"She will take you to our commander," the officer said, pointing out a secretary. "I will wait here—but there he is now!"

Two men strode from a doorway. Desmarais saw Sayed Ahamed and another man she knew as Akbar, an English-speaking Shia who worked closely with Powell the Marine. Akbar had traveled with Desmarais and Powell to Mexico.

Turning away, Desmarais laid her credentials on the secretary's desk. She tossed her head slightly, causing her shoulder-length black hair to fall forward, screening her face. Commander Ahamed and Akbar continued into the corridor.

But Akbar had recognized her. He told his commander, "That woman in there. She says she is a Canadian journalist. But she works for the Soviets."

"That one? Who comes to interview me?"

"Kill her. Arrange her death. In America, we would have executed her, except for the Mexicans. The Mexicans would not allow it, even though she spies for the Soviets."

"I will consider it. Could she be looking for the Americans?"

"Question her. It does not matter if she survives."

"I will consider it. Good fortune on your attack—go. I will deal with the woman."

"GENTLEMEN," Powell began. "Here we have a convoy of very common, nondescript, semiarmored vehicles carrying sufficient firepower to surprise and overwhelm all checkpoints without armored or aircraft support."

Like a television used-car salesman, Powell moved along a line of a Land Rover, a Mercedes troop truck and a semitruck and trailer. "These two, the Rover and the Mercedes, are standard transportation for the Syrian army, and are still marked accordingly. However, the .50-caliber machine gun and the fully automatic grenade launcher are not stock. They—"

"An MK-19?" Lyons interrupted. "Forty millimeter?"

"Four hundred rounds per minute, range of sixteen hundred meters. Very special, just for you. This Mercedes—you see them everywhere. And that truck and trailer—Akbar and his uncles ship tons of contraband a week into Damascus, using exactly that truck. The militias, the Syrian army soldiers, the border guards all know that truck because they always wait for it with their palms out for their cut of the cash.''

''Smuggling?'' Gadgets asked. ''Like what?''

''Well, take a look.'' Powell opened the doors at the rear of the truck.

Stacked from the deck to the roof, from side panel to side panel, were boxes of familiar mass-market products: detergents, hand soaps, toothpaste, designer jeans, kitchen and household appliances and junk food. Like blocks in a Chinese puzzle, the boxes had been fitted into the trailer to utilize every cubic centimeter.

''There it is,'' Powell jived. ''The answer to the Peoples' Revolution. Syria can't get it from the Soviets, so they get it from the United States and Europe, via Lebanon. Via Akbar's family. Via about ten thousand different smugglers. It comes in by boat, like the one you dudes came on, then moves through Beirut to Damascus, then to Iraq and Iran, even into Russia and Afghanistan. Sometimes the trucks carry stuff like this, other times it's video recorders and TVs and videocassettes. Sometimes it's refrigerators and air conditioners.''

''Where will we ride?'' Blancanales asked.

''Inside, up front.''

''Will that trash stop bullets?'' Lyons pointed at the boxes. ''I'm not going to hide in there waiting for an AK slug to punch through.''

"That 'trash' is not what it seems. The first layer is merchandise, for payoffs and giveaways. Then there's a layer of steel, then sandbags. Won't stop artillery or rockets, but you'll be safe from rifles and machine guns and lightweight shrapnel."

"I don't like it," Lyons told him. "It isn't my style to hide out while other people take point for me. It's my mission; I'll take the risks."

Powell grinned. "I can understand that. I know you. But I didn't know you would be on the mission when I came up with this concept. I thought it would be the standard-issue agent out of Washington. You know, 'Where's my limo? Where's my hotel? Why don't these dirty people speak English?' That kind of clown. However, you could get into it. Watch this."

He banged on the trailer and stepped back. Where meter-high black lettering had been painted on the side, panels opened and the barrel of an automatic rifle emerged. A militiaman peered out at the Americans.

Powell led them to the cab. Above the roof, machine-gun barrels appeared. The gunports on the sides and front made the trailer into a moving bunker.

"Boom-boom!" A fighter called out. "Kill Syrians!"

Lyons laughed. "Motivated!"

"That's very good for us," Blancanales commented. "But what about the driver? He'll be totally exposed."

Opening the driver's door, Powell pointed to steel plates reinforcing the doors and firewall and flipped down sun visors made of steel. Other plates flipped up

over the side windows and windshield, forming a slit
only a hand's width wide.

"Won't stop a rocket," Powell told them. "But it
stops bullets and shrapnel."

"Okay," Gadgets said, grinning. "Supercool. But
what about the tires?"

"They're flat-proof. They've got solid inner cores."

"Oh, man!" Gadgets kicked a tire. "You got it covered! How'd you do this in a week?"

Powell shook his head. "Didn't do it in a week. Remember, this war's been going on for ten years.
Akbar's family has been running toothpaste and disco
jeans into Syria since '78. How do you think Shias
could afford to send a son to the University of Califor-
nia?"

"Free enterprise," Blancanales said, nodding. "But
aren't they risking their connections if they take an
American kill squad into Syrian territory?"

"Pol," said the Marine captain, using the Puerto
Rican's code name. "These people think you guys are
okay. Because you're coming here to fight for them, to
get the Syrians out of their country so that it won't be
one more Soviet slave state. No one's talking any
phony peacekeeping missions, none of you are helping
those fascist Maronites. You're here to fight the
enemies of Lebanon. Don't you worry about them losing their connections. They're worried about losing
their country. The people here will do anything to
make this a success."

A man ran from the stairwell toward them. Akbar
talked quickly with Powell.

Then Powell told Able Team, "That Commie bitch

Desmarais is here. And guess what the Shia security saw in her passport? Entry and exit stamps for the U.S. of A. via La Guardia, then Cyprus, then Beirut. Anybody you know been to New York and Cyprus on their way here?''

Able Team glanced at one another. Gadgets answered for his partners. ''Just us tourists.''

8

Surrounded by cars of bodyguards, Sayed Ahamed and Anne Desmarais toured the hills of Beirut. The intermittent shellfire had cleared the roads of traffic. Only military vehicles braved the danger.

But few shells fell near the city or the surrounding villages. The unidentified forces fighting with artillery and small arms along the Beirut-Damascus highway did not fire at the Lebanese militias. They bombarded other unknown forces. Shells and rockets screamed across the dark sky.

As the war came, the weather changed. The chill, bright afternoon had faded as the onrushing storm front darkened the sky. For hours since leaving headquarters, they had driven through the cold winds, interviewing field officers and lookouts. Sometimes they talked with peasants. But they learned nothing of the fighting. Now snow flurries swirled around the limousine. Desmarais looked out at a landscape of grays and black touched by smears of green and startling white.

Rockets streaked into a distant mountain amid a flash of red. But no rockets threatened the line of cars carrying Ahamed and the Canadian journalist back to Beirut.

"But there must be some information on the fighting," Desmarais insisted to Ahamed.

"The Syrian radio reports nothing. The telephones are dead. My officers have attempted even to contact the extremist groups in the Bekaa. But there seems to be a jamming operation in progress. Many voices, many noises on all the radio frequencies. Total chaos. Even though the fighting is in my country, I know nothing."

"Not even rumors?"

"There are always rumors!" The debonair militia chieftain laughed. "Rumors are nothing, less than nothing, for the stories confuse the people and obscure the truth."

"But what of the stories of the Zionist gangs attacking the Syrian positions?"

"Is this a question for your newspaper? Or a joke? What Zionist gangs? Do you mean the Israelis? Why would the Israelis attack the Syrians?"

"To start another war."

"Why would they start another war? Don't they have enough problems now?"

"The Americans pay the Zionist gangs to make trouble and war. Then the Americans intervene."

"Who tells you these stories?" Ahamed leaned close to her. "Do you listen to Radio Moscow? You can tell me. The driver cannot hear or see through the glass." He glanced to the tinted, bulletproof partition dividing the front from the rear.

"No, not Radio Moscow. I listen to the people of Beirut. I listen to the lies of Zionists and the Yankee imperialists."

As Ahamed moved closer, she became very aware of the expensive smuggled cologne he wore. For this ride

with her into the hills, he had worn his gold rings and
Rolex wristwatch, a perfectly tailored uniform and a
beret set at a rakish angle on his head. Did he mean to
impress the foreign journalist with his elegance?

Or to seduce her?

She considered the value of an affair with Sayed
Ahamed. As one of the most effective militia com-
manders—a chieftain who not only controlled hundreds of trained fighters but also led them to decisive
victories against opponents of his Shia people—he had
earned the respect of all the other militias operating in
Beirut. More, he combined his military knowledge and
élan with the skills of politics. When he spoke for the
Shias, all other factions listened.

To the citizens of Beirut, Ahamed represented the
values of strength and faith. He might emerge as a national leader in the moderate government of conciliation.

An intimate involvement with Sayed Ahamed would
advance her career as journalist and as Soviet agent.

He whispered again, his words warm on her ear.
"Why do you not listen to me? I can tell you so much
more. Always the journalists come and question, but
then they print what they believe, what they imagine,
not what I say. But you, intelligent. . .and so very pretty. . . ."

She laughed, putting her head back so that he could
look at her throat and down her blouse. "You must be
desperate for a press release. . . ."

He kissed her throat, exactly as she intended. A
strong hand touched a breast, stroked her body. She
glanced to the driver, to be sure he faced forward. She

could see only the silhouette of his head as he drove, the lights of cars and buildings causing his shadow on the bulletproof partition to shift and leap.

How should she develop this romance? Should she now push away the Shia commander's hands and pretend he had gone too far? Or should she fake a wild passion?

He spoke beautiful French. He had undoubtedly visited France, perhaps studied in a university there, perhaps lived there for years. What had been his experience with French girls? Had he known only prostitutes? Or had he attempted to bed the good Catholic girls, the sisters of his French friends? As a foreigner, he had certainly encountered French prejudice and chauvinism. The girls in their minis and alluring fashions would flirt, but would they go further?

She did not have time to play a game. The American terror team had come to Beirut to meet Powell, the ex-Marine, the wild-eyed killer of her Soviet and Syrian brothers in struggle. Powell worked with Sayed Ahamed. If she hoped to locate and mark Powell for death, she must overwhelm Ahamed.

Ahamed must dream and rave for his new conquest, his French-speaking Canadian mistress, the mysterious journalist.

Desmarais returned his kisses, her body shifting, moving against him, pushing him back against the door. She covered his mouth with hers, waged a battle of tongues before putting her lips to his throat and tasting the bitter-salt of his cologne and sweat, feeling the fine stubble of his beard against her face.

He's already hard, she thought, feeling steel against

her thigh. She reached down to stroke him, found his holstered pistol. She pushed the weapon to the side. As she touched him, she felt him shudder. Kissing his throat, his chest, she slid down.

As she unbuttoned his pants, he watched the dark streets pass. No matter how distant the fighting, no civilians risked the streets. He knew the Syrians fought one another, but the radio and television stations did not carry that information. The announcers repeated only the rumors of a Syrian civil war and the assurances of the Council of Conciliation. The people of Beirut had gone to the uncertain safety of their shelters to listen to their radios and wait. After ten years of war, they disregarded rumors and assurances and went underground when they heard distant shellfire.

She mouthed him and clenched at him. Her head went up and down. Ahamed almost yawned. He gripped her head in both hands and guided her up and down. He did not want her to see him looking at his watch. Checking the time, he realized he should concentrate on this pathetic sex act because if he did not ejaculate quickly she might expect him to join her in her hotel room. And he had other appointments. Already, he had wasted hours to get the woman out of Beirut while Akbar and Powell completed their preparations and departed. Perhaps he should have killed her in the hills. That would have spared him the indignity of a blood test.

The thought of the millions of syphilis spirochetes now writhing and reproducing on his lips after kissing this Soviet whore and the millions more invading his genitals made him shudder with disgust. The woman mistook the shudder as ecstasy and redoubled her fervor.

Get it over with, Ahamed silently screamed.
Nauseated, he looked out at the boulevard and saw a
Syrian Land Rover pass. A Mercedes troop truck fol-
lowed, then a truck and trailer.

Akbar, Powell and the other Americans! On their
way out of Beirut!

The neon lights of the hotel appeared. Ahamed
saw the lead car swerve into the traffic circle, then
the limo. The doorman approached. Ahamed knotted
his hands in Desmarais's hair to guide and distract
her.

As the doorman reached for the handle of the opposite door, Ahamed shoved the woman away and
unlocked the door. Her lips gleaming with saliva, Desmarais clutched at his thighs, trying to pull his body
down, to drive his rigid organ again into her mouth, and
Ahamed pushed her out of the vehicle.

The doorman caught her. Slapping the partition,
Ahamed shouted to the driver, "Go!"

Gasping, blinking against the lights of the hotel's entry, Desmarais sat in the gutter and watched the limousine speed away. The doorman, who had seen into
the limousine, stared at her. Desmarais twisted out of
his hands and stood up. Wiping her mouth, she hurried
to the hotel entrance.

As she stalked through the doorway, she turned and
saw the doorman talking with a bellboy. The doorman
mimicked an erect penis with his fist and thumb, then
two men burst into laughter. They watched her watching them and laughed.

"Miss Desmarais!"

Livid, she raged with thoughts of revenge. A car-bombing of the hotel? Assassinate the doorman? An air strike on the headquarters of Ahamed?

She turned and instantly recognized the stoop-shouldered bear of a man at the telephones. Zhgenti! He motioned her to approach. A dark, peasant-faced man from a southern republic of the Soviet Union, he passed without notice among the dark peoples of the Middle East. Only his Slavic accent and faulty French and Arabic betrayed him. But he more than qualified for a field operative with his passion for murder. The KGB would not have sent him for information.

They sat together. Desmarais did not waste time on greetings. "What happened?"

"The Americans destroyed the cruiser. All my men and the Palestinians died. Not a trace left."

"How could that—"

"How does not matter! Why do you not already know this? All day you have been out, searching for that other American. They are with him. Did you find them?"

"No. I tried to get the information from Sayed Ahamed, the commander of the militia gang that Powell—"

"Tried to suck the information from him!" Zhgenti hissed with anger, his eyes narrowing to slits. "I was here. I looked and I saw a whore thrown out of a limousine. The whore was you. Is that how you gain your information? Servicing Arabs in the backs of their limousines? Like a Soho street girl? I should send you to work for the English. But we need you now. Go—"

"For what?"

"Take orders, whore!" Zhgenti never allowed his

voice to rise above a whisper. He sounded like a snake. He looked like a snake. Desmarais did not dare interrupt him again. "You go to your room. Get warm clothing. And whatever other whore things you need to pass as a journalist. You failed and now we must go to the Bekaa to look for the Americans. Go! Now, or I put a bullet in your head. And not my big bullet. I will give you one that will splatter your brains!"

Desmarais stumbled to an elevator, pounded the button. She had no doubt that Zhgenti would do as he threatened. As she waited, she looked back. Zhgenti pushed through the hotel doors.

She saw the two vans waiting in the traffic circle, the broad faces of Soviets in them. Other passengers appeared to be Palestinian contract soldiers. The spray-painted sides of the vans identified them as newsmen in English, French, Arabic and Farsi. But she knew they could not be television technicians. Zhgenti did not travel for news. He traveled to kill.

The elevator took her to her floor. Running to her room, she quickly packed her overnight bag with underwear and shirts and film.

In her warmest trench coat, she ran back to the elevator, summoned it. Her overnight bag bounced against her, clinking against the camera under her coat. She glanced at herself in a mirror as she waited. With a scarf protecting her throat and a fur hat on her head, she certainly looked the role of the young woman journalist.

Only four years before, she had been a struggling writer of romance novels, typing and retyping manuscripts, hoping for a sale but earning only rejections.

Desperate to make the right connections, she had left Quebec for a job in Toronto as a copy editor at a romance publisher, correcting the manuscripts of other struggling writers. But she never sold her writing until she wrote a column for a leftist newsletter.

Her editorials denouncing acid rain as an imperialist plot of American transnational corporations earned a call from a man with an accent. He asked her to continue writing her anti-American tirades.

Checks came. Then airline tickets with a typed list of names and addresses. She churned out controversial interviews and stories that appeared on the op-ed pages of some of the best newspapers. After she'd had a year of excellent sales, a representative of the Soviet Union approached her with an offer too good to refuse. She had no objections to working for the Soviets.

She loathed Americans and the United States.

9

Wearing the uniform of a Soviet advisor to the Syrian army, Carl Lyons rode in the open back of the Mercedes troop transport with two Shia militiamen in Syrian uniforms. Akbar and Hussein, in the cab, also wore Syrian uniforms. Syrian army regulation gloves, coats, wool scarves and blankets protected them from the snowstorm. The truck also matched the vehicles of the Syrian forces.

They rode in silence, their weapons in their hands. Beside Lyons, a Browning .50-caliber machine gun stood ready on its pedestal, a belt of armor-piercing cartridges in place. An M-79 grenade launcher and a bandolier of 40mm grenades hung from the pedestal. Black plastic secured with a neoprene snap cord concealed both weapons: Syrian forces did not employ the American-made weapons.

The disguises would be the key to passing through most checkpoints. But if questioned, Hussein carried perfect forgeries of military travel orders.

A hundred meters ahead, Powell and two other Shias rode point in the Land Rover. Powell wore a Soviet uniform; the Shias wore Syrian uniforms and carried military documents. Plastic covered the MK-19 40mm grenade launcher mounted in the back of the

Rover, where loaded RPGs stood ready. Powell needed only to twist off the safety-cap wires, cock the launcher and fire the rockets.

Last in the convoy, Blancanales and Gadgets enjoyed the warmth of the trailer as they manned a second set of heavy weapons, another Browning .50-caliber and another MK-19. But these launchers and other weapons would be used only if their documents and disguises failed.

A Shia vehicle passed them without a word. The militiamen stared at the passing Syrians and Soviets with open hatred. Their officer waved; he was the only one who knew that Shias drove the Rover and trucks.

Continuing east, the convoy left all life behind. Their headlights revealed abandoned vehicles and deserted villages. Far away in the storm and night, the incomprehensible war continued. Rockets and shellfire flashed on distant positions. Flares seared the storm clouds.

Able Team's three hand-radios buzzed. Powell spoke to the other Americans through a fourth NSA unit. "Gentlemen, we are now in it. I am monitoring the frequencies on a Syrian army radio, and I am hearing very scary things. There are at least three different army factions calling one another traitors and usurpers. They are fighting one another and—here's the joke—they are also engaging with forces of the Muslim Brotherhood. I guessed the political factionalism. But the Muslim Brotherhood is something else.

"Last time the Brotherhood rebelled, they seized and defended the city of Hama against battalions of the best Syrian troops. The Syrians destroyed the city. A total slaughter. Maybe twenty thousand, thirty thousand people killed: no one will ever know. If the Brotherhood is back, they're back in force and they're out for revenge.

"I tell you," Powell continued, "the Brotherhood's more than I planned on. Why don't you three reconsider this mission. If you want to go on, okay. But it ain't too late to go back. We could wait for the politics and religion to get straight."

Lyons answered immediately. "We can't. If those missiles get out, we'll have to search every ship and every plane between here and the White House to find them. I say we go."

"How long a wait are you proposing?" Blancanales asked Powell.

"Could be a few days, could be a few weeks before—"

"Forget it!" Lyons interrupted.

"Why stop?" Gadgets asked. "Look at all those fireworks! It's the Fourth of July everywhere."

"We can't risk a delay of weeks," Blancanales concluded. "A few hours, a day perhaps...."

"Then it's unanimous." Powell sighed. "I hoped you cowboys would exercise discretion, as they say. We just might be going into a four-way free-fire zone."

The others waited for Gadgets' jive line, but the electronics wizard said nothing. He just held down the transmit key and laughed.

In the back of the troop truck, Lyons lost patience with his partner and pocketed the radio. He glanced at the two Shia militiamen riding with him. In the darkness, he could not see their faces. Blankets over their legs and feet, they watched the distant firefights. Both held Soviet PKM belt-fed machine guns, the muzzles pointing through the slats of the truck. Their rifles, folding-stock Kalashnikovs, hung from the inner slats, clattering with every bump in the road.

Four-way free-fire zone, Lyons thought. Then he realized why Gadgets laughed. Able Team always went into uncontrolled zones. In New York City or El Salvador or the Bekaa, always the same—

The two militiamen started. Lyons heard the sound also. The not-so-distant thunking of mortar tubes. They had ten to twenty seconds before the mortars hit.

Lyons slipped his Konzak sling over his head and cinched the shotgun diagonally across his back. Standing in the freezing wind, he pulled the plastic sheet off the Browning and secured it to the pedestal with the neoprene snap cord. Ahead, he saw Powell swiveling the MK-19, looking for a target.

White light seared the night. High above the highway, a magnesium flare swung on a miniature parachute.

Mortar impacts flashed ahead, the booms of the explosions coming an instant later. Another flare blazed overhead. A random pattern of mortar hits scored the highway and the roadside, balls of smoke hanging in the night. Spent shrapnel rattled off the truck. Hot metal burned Lyons's neck. He tore at his scarf and a jagged bit of iron fell out.

Switching off their headlights, the drivers of the three vehicles drove by the white flares.

The Land Rover shot through the pall of smoke.

Seconds behind, the Mercedes troop truck bumped over the broken asphalt. Then a mortar exploded behind the truck, and dirt and rocks and iron pocked the wooden slats. A scrape appeared in the cab in front of Lyons.

From a rise to the north approximately three hundred meters away, a rocket launcher flashed, and an instant later the RPG warhead passed behind the Rover and exploded in a long streak on the earth. Powell answered with 40mm grenades, firing single grenades to find the range, then dropping a burst of alternating high-explosive and white phosphorous grenades on the position. Lyons sighted the Browning and raked the ridge with .50-caliber slugs as the Shias behind him fired bursts from their PKM machine guns. Tracers from the ridge and the convoy crossed.

One sparking point moved. An automatic weapon fired from a vehicle, the line of tracers going wild as the vehicle bumped and lurched over a rutted track. Another flare burst into white glare and Lyons saw a Japanese truck speeding for the highway in an attempt to cut them off. A soldier fired a pedestal-mounted machine gun from the back of the truck.

Lyons swung the Browning around and fired. The first burst went low, and a single tracer skipped off the rocks, pinwheeling away into the storm clouds. Adjusting his aim, Lyons saw a tracer disappear into the truck. He held down the Browning's button and counted out ten rounds.

The truck veered to the right and overturned. Powell sighted on the overturned truck and fired a 3-shot burst of 40mm, hitting it with high-explosive, white phosphorous, then high ex again. Spilled gasoline sheetflamed.

Returning his aim to the ridge, Powell fired for area effect. High-ex flashes and white chemical fire splashed the ridge, than a ball of orange petroleum flame surged into the sky as he hit another vehicle.

Lyons saw the silhouettes of a mortar crew and sighted the Browning. A red line of tracers touched the silhouettes. Powell found the crew with a 40mm burst.

No more mortars came. Individual riflemen fired on the convoy, slugs intermittently punching into the wood sidings of the troop truck. All the firing stopped as they left the ambush behind.

Lyons covered the Browning, then glanced back to the Shia militiamen. In the dying flarelight, the leather-faced, middle-aged men grinned and gave Lyons the V for victory. Lyons keyed his hand-radio. "Everyone okay?"

"No problems here," Blancanales responded. "Anyone know who fired at us?"

"You mean," Powell answered, "did we take names? Fuck, no. Ain't killing them good enough?"

"We didn't even get a shot off!" Gadgets complained. "Our guns only cover the road—"

"Hey, Wizard," Powell drawled in his true East Texas dialect. "You just wait. I think you'll get your chance. Any minute now."

A KILOMETER PAST KAHHALE, a Lebanese army armored personnel carrier blocked the highway. A soldier with a flashlight told the Palestinian drivers of the vans to return to Beirut. Other soldiers manned the machine guns of the APC. Zhgenti did not challenge the orders. He told the drivers to find a way around the roadblock.

A few minutes later, as the vans bumped over a dirt sideroad, Zhgenti cursed. "Storms, revolutions, whores and pretty little soldiers—I must kill those Americans and the world is against me. My superiors will not listen to excuses. What a mess. What a sorry mess this is!"

"Illovich is the one," Desmarais snapped back at the Soviet. "He had them prisoner. He wanted a propaganda event. What a dreamer that old man is. I said he must kill them while he had them because they were vile, tricky, fascist bastards who'd do anything, stop at nothing—"

"Not like you, eh?" Zhgenti leered. "My tricky little Canadian."

The vans came to a village devastated by artillery. No lights showed from the windows of the remaining houses. Nothing moved on the streets of frozen mud. As the vans followed the narrow road, their headlights illuminated pathetic vignettes: bundles of rags and stiff hands, staring faces beneath shrapnel-pocked walls; a Syrian army truck that had taken a direct hit, scorched corpses and skeletons hanging from the flame-blackened hulk; a peasant wagon of belongings still hitched to a frozen mule.

A stout Muslim woman waved to them. Inside Zhgenti's van, rifle and submachine gun safeties clicked off. The woman, using an old blanket as a *chador*, stood at a crossroad. Behind her, a form wrapped in blankets lay on the snow. The woman ran wailing to the Zhgenti's van.

"Ask her which road will take us to the Bekaa," the Soviet told the driver.

The Palestinian shouted down her wailing. He questioned her repeatedly. Finally she pointed to the eastern road. The driver turned to Zhgenti.

"Her husband's wounded. She's begging us to take her to the highway. Or he'll die."

Zhgenti rolled down his window. Pointing an Uzi with one hand, he fired a burst into the blanket-wrapped old man. An arm reached up and clawed the air.

The old Muslim woman shrieked and beat at the van's door. Laughing, the Soviets and Palestinians fired point-blank into her face. She fell back and sat on the snow, blood gushing from enormous wounds to her head. Zhgenti leaned out and fired a long burst that spilled the old woman's brains. Smiling, displaying all the porcelain and stainless steel of his teeth, the Soviet turned to Desmarais. "Remember, my little French Canadian. Never let yourself forget that I am also a vile, vicious bastard who stops at nothing."

Shuddering with the horror, not opening her eyes, Desmarais answered. "I know, I will not forget."

PRETENDING TO SLEEP, Lyons stayed low in the back of the troop truck. He held his Konzak assault shotgun under the blanket covering him.

The Syrians paced around the trucks and Rover. Lyons heard Powell talking in Arabic, followed by Arabic voices shouting back and forth, then boots hitting the road. Someone strode away—the boots splashed through the mud beside the asphalt, continued a few more steps. Powell had gone to the sand-bagged bunker at the side of the highway.

Clicks came from his hand-radio but Lyons did not dare move a hand to return them, not while Syrian sentries surrounded them. Voices came from the bunker. Then the boots returned and the Rover's engine gunned. Hussein clashed the gears as he shifted and then the troop truck moved. Behind the truck, the diesel of the semi roared.

Lyons finally lowered the blanket from his face. Only dark hills and snow surrounded them. His hand-radio clicked again.

"How'd we get through that?" Gadgets asked.

"I don't know," Lyons told his partner. "I kept a blanket over my head. Ask the Marine. I heard him walk into the guardhouse and talk with someone."

Powell came on with a laugh. "Hey, don't get spooked. I told you this would be tight. It's just started, you hear me?"

"What went on in the guardhouse?" Lyons asked.

"The officer on duty questioned me. Wanted to know all about us. Why we'd risk being on the road tonight, why I, a Soviet, would be with the convoy and what was in the truck—"

"What'd you tell him?" Gadgets interrupted.

"Hey, is it my job to talk the news? I told him straight out: 'It's a secret.'"

10

In the underground factory, Syrian technicians completed final checks of the Soviet BM-240mm rocket-firing systems. They shouted questions and answers to one another, some gathered around the cargo containers, others inside them. Senior technicians watched the digital displays of instruments that monitored the firing circuits.

Workers were moving everywhere in the factory. Mechanics checked the bolts securing the cargo containers to the flatbed trailers. Clerks passed the workbenches to inventory machines and tools. Skiploaders moved crates from the workshops to the far walls, stacking them for later transport.

At the steel doors to the underground complex of offices and workshops, groups of soldiers with slung Kalashnikovs stood talking of the political war and the attack by the Muslim Brotherhood. As guards for the trucks, the soldiers would not begin their duties until the convoy of rockets left for America.

Colonel Ali Dastgerdi directed every detail of the final assembly.

Now, in the last hours of the greatest project of his career, after years of work, Dastgerdi would not allow some petty distraction of a technician to rob him of victory. He stood behind the engineers as they compared the test impulses to the amperage specified in the manuals. He watched the electrical technicians check the conduits leading into the trailers. He climbed inside each flatbed trailer and checked the soldering of the firing wires to the fuses of the rockets.

With a workman's ladder, he went to the roofs of the containers and examined the bolts securing the aluminum sheeting to the side walls. Then he touched the release latches to confirm the lubrication of the moving parts.

Nothing could go wrong. He could not accompany the rockets from the underground factory. He could not travel through the Bekaa to the Mediterranean, then to the mid-Atlantic, where the crane ship from Nicaragua would transfer the containers to a freighter for the final segment of the trip to the United States. He could not ride in the trucks transporting the rockets to the capital of the United States.

Every one of thousands of details must be perfect. No qualified personnel would be in the trucks or on the freighters to correct last-minute failures.

From the moment the rockets left the underground factory, the transportation and deployment would be in the hands of untrained and unqualified terrorists, Islamic radicals—Iranians, Lebanese, American Black Muslims—who believed they waged sacred war for the Ayatollah Khomeini. The ignorant, suicidal fanatics could be trusted only to die.

But every possible malfunction had been anticipated.

Simple bolts secured the aluminum roofs of the

cargo containers. Before the trucks carried the containers the last few kilometers to the District of Columbia, the drivers needed only to remove the bolts to prepare for the firing. Then, the release of one latch allowed the roofs to be torn away in the wind, creating a 120 KPH launch vehicle for the rockets.

Duplicate circuits ensured the firing of the rockets. When the unit leader confirmed the transmission of the homing signals, the leader had simply to check the distance from the inauguration, then initiate the firing.

Aluminum-and-plastic-foam antishock cases protected redundant solid-state firing circuits. If damage in transit rendered a pulse generator inoperative, an exact duplicate, wired in parallel, performed the firing.

If American security forces broke the terrorist group responsible for truck-launching the rockets, the action would not defeat the strike. An alternative group stood by to transport the containers up the Potomac as cargo and launch the rockets when they received the homing signals.

Soviet agents in America had distributed the homing-impulse transmitters to ten infiltrators. Though each infiltrator—whether UNESCO bureaucrat, Brazilian professor, New York debutante or limousine chauffeur—thought himself or herself a lone operator, ten would attend the inauguration of the President of the United States.

The infiltrators did not know they would die in a rain of rockets. They had been told the small electronic units monitored and recorded the informal UHF communications of the Presidential staff. Some believed the recordings would be forwarded to newspapers, others that the recordings would be used to embarrass the President.

If the American secret service—by some fantastic blessing of luck—intercepted one or two or five of the infiltrators and confiscated the minitransmitters, it did not matter. The transmitters of the other five infiltrators would guide the rockets to the inauguration. If only one of the ten infiltrators penetrated American security, the one transmitter would be sufficient to guide the rain of Soviet missiles onto the assembly of America's elite.

Following the impulses to the inauguration, the missiles would rain doom upon the President and all the other representatives of America, the doom of high explosives and white phosphorous and nerve gases.

To create prime-time terror for a national viewing audience. To create national rage beyond reason.

The surviving political leaders would not restrain the demands for revenge. No politician would preach restraint or forgiveness. No one could speak against a devastating counterstrike on Iran. America would answer Islamic terror with war.

And the Soviet Union, under the terms of the 1926 mutual defense treaty with Iran, would rush its armored divisions to the rescue of its southern neighbor. America's revenge would create the Soviet Republic of Iran.

Satisfied with the work of his technicians and staff, Colonel Dastgerdi approached the officer heading the detachment of Syrian troops. "When can we leave?"

The Syrian smiled and shrugged. "Only God knows."

"What kind of answer is that?"

"It is all very confused. Our forces face the traitorous forces of the—"

"Don't recite propaganda to me!" Dastgerdi indicated the trucks and flatbed trailers bearing the containers with a sweep of his arm. "These must be transported through the madness."

"True, Colonel. It is madness in the night. The fanatics of the Brotherhood wage war against our country. They strike everywhere. It is terrible."

"When will they be destroyed? Spare me the repeating of what they broadcast. When can this cargo move?"

"Only God knows. Perhaps minutes, perhaps days. The word will come."

ZHGENTI CURSED. After hours of racing through the twisting, ice-slick mountain roads, the vans came to another checkpoint. Here, on the eastern slopes of the Jabal el-Knisse, where the highway led down into the Bekaa, the Syrian army stopped all traffic.

Lines of troop trucks, freight trucks, civilian and military cars and tanks waited for clearance to continue. With a flashlight, Zhgenti checked a map for an alternative route. No roads bypassed the checkpoint.

"Go into the opposite lanes," Zhgenti told the Palestinian driver. "Get past all those trucks. Go up to the Syrians. We cannot wait here all night."

Swinging into the left-hand lane, the driver sped past other vehicles, then jammed on the brakes. Two Syrian soldiers stood in the glare of the headlights, their Kalashnikov rifles aimed at the van's windshield. An officer shouted and motioned the driver back.

"They will not allow it," the Palestinian told Zhgenti.

"Demand to speak to the officer in command. We have clearance for—"

A flash. An explosion rocked the van, the night suddenly a red dawn. Pieces of rock and metal rained down on the roof. Shells screamed down from the storm.

Vehicle chaos came an instant later. Trucks swerved into the open lane. Tanks left the asphalt and ground along the shoulder. Soldiers ran everywhere as shells continued to fall around the traffic jam.

"Drive!" Zhgenti shouted, beating on the driver's back.

The van rolled sideways, the shock of a blast shattering the windows, spraying the interior with thousands of cubes of tempered glass. Continuing through the sideways roll, they saw a ball of flame rising from what had been a truck.

Desmarais screamed as the van rolled. Then the van stopped on its roof and she crawled from the window, her overnight bag clutched in her hand. Standing in the swirling snow and the sudden day, she saw burning hulks and maneuvering vehicles. The wounded were dying under tires and tank treads. Leaking gasoline became streams of fire.

A long, wailing scream drowned out the engines and explosions and shouts. Desmarais realized the scream came from her own throat, as she stood upright in the flames and chaos and death.

Her legs responded to her panic with blind and unreasoning animal flight. Headlights and fire illuminated her path through the rocks and debris. Then came the body-numbing shock of another high-explosive blast, and she hit the asphalt. She ran again, her flight bag banging against her legs with every step.

A troop transport passed her. Brakes squealed, tires smoked as the truck slowed. Headlights behind her—the lights seemed to come from the sky—revealed the empty back of the transport. She threw herself over the boards. Behind her were the searing headlights of a huge truck. Its roaring diesel engine drowned out her whimpering and the screams of the dying along the roadside.

Two soldiers looked across at her. In the back of the transport, the Syrians lay flat, exposing as little as possible of their bodies to the blast and shrapnel of the artillery barrage.

"Journalist!" she screamed, her voice cracking with panic. "Journalist! Journalist!" She repeated the word in French and Arabic. The soldiers ignored her.

The truck accelerated. Scenes of flames and darkness flashed past. A shock rocked the truck, splintered wood, showering her. She looked up to see that a shell fragment had slashed through a thick plank on one side. Tangled in the other slats, the plank shifted and bumped with the lurching of the truck. A soldier who sat against the truck's cab scrambled across the deck and shoved the splintered plank out.

Pausing for an instant, the soldier looked at her. A fur hat and a scarf covered his face, but she saw Caucasian skin and blue eyes. A Russian? He returned to his position near a heavy machine gun and wrapped a blanket around himself as the truck hurtled through the night.

Desmarais called in her basic Arabic to the two Syrian soldiers. "I am a journalist. I go to Damascus. You take me to Damascus?"

"Yes, we go there," one of the Shias replied, nodding.

"Thank you, thank you," she sobbed.

They left the carnage behind. Desmarais put her face to the dirty boards and gasped down breath after breath.

She had survived.

And she had left Zhgenti behind.

An arm's reach away from Desmarais, Carl Lyons whispered into his hand-radio. "We just picked up a hitchhiker. Guess who it is?"

The others heard him laughing.

SHOUTING, CURSING, ZHGENTI led his men through the wreckage. The Palestinians and Soviets of his kill squad had abandoned any pretense of representing a news network. They had taken their weapons and equipment and left the empty cases to burn in the wrecked vans. Now they moved through the flames and swirling snow, hurrying to the safety of the open highway.

Trucks and cars burned around them. Shells continued to fall hundreds of meters to the east as the distant artillery unit walked the 130mm shells along the highway, blasting the blazing trucks and screaming wounded again and again. Secondary explosions sent the twisted wreckage of transports spinning through the night.

Others also tried to put the slaughter behind them. Vehicles somehow untouched wove through the hulks scattered along the highway. Crowded with soldiers, a troop transport low-geared around the tangle of metal that had been a private car before a high-explosive shell reduced it to scattered fenders and burning upholstery. Syrian soldiers left the roadside ditches and sprinted after the transport. Three soldiers managed to clutch the side slats and ride away holding on to the outside of the truck.

"We want a truck!" Zhgenti called out to his squad. "One of these, any one that isn't ruined."

But high explosive and shrapnel had destroyed the vehicles they found. Ignoring the flaming trucks, they checked the vans and trucks that had run off the road in the first chaotic minute of the artillery barrage.

One of the Soviets ran to a small Japanese truck with four-wheel drive. The vehicle showed no damage other than shattered windows. But the interior was filled with torn corpses. A blast of shrapnel had turned the opposite side of the truck into a lattice of perforated fenders and doors, the steel cut to shreds by the high-velocity fragments of a bursting shell. Ignoring the gore inside, the Soviet checked the engine and tires and found that the fragments had totaled the truck.

The squad continued checking trucks until they came to what remained of the Syrian unit that had established the checkpoint.

One of the BMP combat vehicles had taken a direct hit. Nothing remained except the track threads and the slab of armor plating that had formed the undercarriage. The wreckage of the armored vehicle—and the blood-clotted shreds of the crew—lay everywhere.

A second BMP nearby had taken the blast of a shell without apparent damage. However, the soldiers inside had not closed the rear hatches. The high-velocity fragments, like supersonic axes, had ricochetted throughout the interior of the vehicle. Blood flowed from the armored troop carrier.

Zhgenti looked down at a Syrian officer gasping on the asphalt. The dying officer clutched at his open gut, his hands lost in a tangle of intestines.

"Fool!" Zhgenti spat into the Syrian's agony-racked face. "You had to delay me. Don't you understand that some people do not have time for your petty politics?"

Leaving the roadblock commander to die, Zhgenti directed his men to spread out. He raised his Uzi above his head and shouted, "The next one that comes through is ours! Take it!"

11

Only a flashlight lit the interior of the sandbag bunker inside the trailer. Desmarais sat on the floor as Blancanales questioned her.

For the first time since the Canadian journalist-cum-Soviet agent had sought out Powell and become involved with the American pursuit of the terrorists, Desmarais spoke truthfully. She no longer pretended to be a journalist. She no longer preached her anti-American politics. She no longer taunted the American antiterrorist fighters.

Chaos and luck had defeated her. The game of deceit had ended. Now she hoped only for survival.

"The assignment to the rocket group came like all the others. My director called and briefed me, and then all the materials and tickets and names of contacts came in the mail. I was surprised when I saw that I would be investigating Soviets, but I did not question the assignment—"

"All the other times," Blancanales interrupted to clarify the point. "The director—the voice on the telephone—sent you against Americans?"

"Yes. Stories about American activities for the Canadian and European newspapers, sometimes for Soviet newspapers. But this time I used my job only for cover. I knew my director would not want a story published about these Iranians and Syrians. But I followed it—''

"Why were you certain?" Blancanales asked.

"Because the Syrians are allies of the Soviet Union. And I saw that they were working together with the Iranian fundamentalists. I did not learn what the project would be, but it involved only terrorist groups. It had to be terrorism. When the Iranians killed the CIA men in Beirut, that could be a story. I investigated that as if I were writing a story. That took me to Powell. I knew Shabakkar—he is the fighter for the creation of the Black Nation of Islam in North America—and Shabakkar said he would speak with Powell, but it was a trap and the Iranians took me—''

"Did they actually rape you? Or was that another—''

"Yes! I wish it had been staged. Oshakkar betrayed me to those animals. They intended to kill me but I killed them."

"And what of the information you claimed to have overheard between the Libyan and the Nicaraguan?''

"That was talk of the rockets, that they would be flown in and then transported in trucks. But I would not have told you Americans that, not until I discussed the information with Illovich."

"You called ahead to Illovich?"

"Of course. I called the Soviet embassy in Mexico, I gave them my code number and they connected me to Illovich. He took over from there."

"What can you tell us about Illovich?"

"He is KGB."

"No shit?" Gadgets laughed. He sat on a box of

40mm grenades, his feet on the MK-19 launcher. "What a revelation. I got to write that one down. Tell us something we don't know."

"Easy, partner," Blancanales cautioned. "Miss, what did he know of the rockets?"

"Nothing."

"What did he know when you arrived? He had two days to consult with Moscow."

"He knew nothing. He said it was very important that the terrorists be destroyed. He sent his men against the Iranians and you killed them all. That was when you captured us."

"What happened after . . . after you escaped?"

"We returned to Mexico City. We learned that you Americans had destroyed the terrorists. And that was that."

"But then you followed us again. How did that happen?"

"I received a call from my director. Because I knew your team by sight and could identify you, they told me to follow you."

"You spotted us on Cyprus."

Desmarais did not answer.

"We know you followed us to Cyprus. And our boat was attacked. Did you identify us there for a hit squad?"

"Yes."

"And then you came to Lebanon?"

"To find Powell."

"Why is Powell important?"

"He is an American. He is CIA—"

"Wow, he's an American!" Gadgets interrupted

again. "What do you got against us? What is your problem?"

"You Americans! You ignore my country, you dominate all the hemisphere—Quebec, Canada, all the nations. You force your corporate fascist culture on us. Of course I oppose you. All the Quebecois hate you. Even the Anglos of Canada. We will someday rise against you."

"How did you get out here?"

"I followed you."

"Alone! You came into this insane war alone?"

"No."

Staring at the floor, the young woman did not speak for a moment. In the silence, they heard the droning of the diesel engine and the endless sound of tires on asphalt. Then she looked up, her eyes studying Blancanales. She spoke again.

"I have many documents from the Syrians. I persuaded some soldiers to take me to Damascus. And then in the shelling, they all died. I jumped out to take photos and then a shell hit the truck and they all died. It was so terrible. Only boys. . . ."

Her voice died away.

"Thank you," Blancanales said. "For the information. I hope we can help you. At least we can help you get safely out of the war." He crossed the trailer and sat on the floor. Aware that Desmarais heard what he said, he spoke softly into his hand-radio. "Ironman, Powell, I've questioned her. None of it really helps. Except one thing. Remember what our pilot friend told us about where the courier went? Said it was an interesting detail?"

Blancanales put the radio against his ear to muffle his partner's voice, so that only he could hear. "Yeah, about Iraq. You got info on that?"

Blancanales plugged in the earphone attachment. Now the prisoner could hear only his words. "Yeah, about that. Indirectly. The KGB has no idea about what's going on with the rockets."

"She says. She says all kinds of things. Anything else she said?"

"Nothing we couldn't have guessed."

"So what do we do with her now?"

"She goes with us, then we take her out."

Powell's voice joined them. Shouting over the wind rush in the open Rover, he told them. "I got a solution for our Soviet problem. Let her walk out."

"This isn't Mexico," Blancanales countered. "She'll die out there."

"She's Canadian," Powell countered. "She can handle the snow."

"She set you up for execution," Lyons reminded Blancanales.

Speaking slightly louder so that his prisoner overheard, Blancanales stated, "I told her we would help her get out of this insanity. My word is my word."

Powell laughed, the sound a mad cackle in the road noise. "Think she'd keep her word to you?"

"I gave my word. Period."

In the back of the troop transport, Lyons jammed his hand-radio back into the pocket of his Soviet army greatcoat. He clutched the blanket tight around his face and shoulders and stood up. Squinting against the freezing wind, he peered into the darkness.

Snow swirled in the headlights of the Land Rover and the Mercedes troop transport. But beyond the wide asphalt band of the modern highway, the night and storm reclaimed the Bekaa. They passed dark houses and villages, no lights showing from windows or shops, even the streetlights dark. Fighting continued in the distance, sparks of light marking fights where soldiers and fanatics—and innocent Lebanese—died for the incomprehensible politics of Syria.

Other headlights appeared behind them, and a Syrian troop convoy passed the American convoy. The Syrian drivers, disregarding the falling snow and slick roads, swerved into the opposing lanes and passed at a suicidal 120 kilometers per hour. Lyons waved to the soldiers in the backs of the trucks. They did not return the waves. Crouched in the transports, wrapped in plastic, they stared at him, their faces sullen. The Syrian convoy continued into the distance, the red points of the taillights finally lost in the night.

A scene of recent combat appeared. None of the Shia drivers even slowed. Ahead, Lyons saw Powell swivel the MK-19 grenade launcher to cover the village and burning vehicles. But no firing came from the defeated.

Soviet armored personnel carriers had assaulted a cluster of houses. Only broken stone and the stink of smoldering fires remained of the village. The gutted hulks of three APCs indicated the victors had suffered heavy casualties in the attack. A light frosting of snow covered the wild circles and zigzagging ruts left by the maneuvering vehicles. The snow also covered the anonymous dead sprawled where they fell. Nothing moved now.

A few kilometers farther, the Rover slowed. Lyons reached for his hand-radio and Powell explained, "No problem, tourists. Just a detour. The Syrians are putting out a call for their forces to assemble. According to our maps, the coordinates are a major highway intersection up ahead. So we're taking a side road. It'll cost only a few minutes."

"How's the war going?" Lyons asked.

"Which one? Syria versus Syria? Syria versus the Brotherhood? Or Syria versus the Iranians and Libyans?"

"The Iranians and Libyans are in it now?"

"Doesn't affect us. The Iranians and Libyans are up by Baalbek. A radio station came on and announced a rising of the Islamic masses. Announced the creation of an Islamic republic in alliance with Khaddafi and the Ayatollah. And the Syrians seem to be stomping the shit out of them. There's artillery officers up there calling down fire-for-effect you cannot believe. I don't think Baalbek will be there tomorrow."

Lyons laughed. "Why should I care what's there? What about in the area of the village?"

"Continuing artillery exchanges. And on the highway to Damascus, Syrian units loyal to the president report conflict with both rebel units and the Brotherhood. In short, free-fire politics all the way to Damascus."

At a side road, the Rover and trucks left the highway and drove south. They maintained a steady, safe speed. Undisturbed snow on the asphalt indicated no other vehicles had used the road in the previous hour or more.

Dark, lifeless farms and fields lay on both sides of the road. But no one had fought there. They drove on through the deserted but peaceful area. Lyons watched the quiet houses, his hands holding the blanket, not the grips of the Browning .50-caliber. The Shia militiamen kept watch also, but they kept their hands on their machine guns.

The peace ended with a roar like a thousand freight trains screaming through the night. Lyons grabbed the Browning. But the Able Team convoy was not the target.

Above, rockets arched through the clouds, then streaked down somewhere to the north. The overhanging storm clouds reflected flashes, the black clouds suddenly a somber red. A rolling, resounding thunder came.

"Katyushas," one of the Shias told Lyons. Then his hand-radio buzzed.

"You cowboys ever seen a rocket barrage before?" Powell asked. "That's what's happening. Guess the opposition monitors the Syrian radios, too."

Gadgets spoke next. "*Soo* glad you made that detour."

"And we're going to make another one," Powell emphasized. "Put some distance between us and them."

Another wave of rockets screamed through the night. Seconds later came the sheet thunder of the explosions.

Approaching another intersection, the Rover turned south. Headlights appeared. Lyons saw Powell salute. A clanking line of Soviet BMT armored personnel carriers escorted by T-62 tanks passed. Playing the role of a Soviet, Lyons also saluted the passing armored column. A blond tank commander, standing in the turret hatch, returned Lyons's salute.

The Rover continued south. They passed farms and walled orchards. Looking back, Lyons saw a horizon of orange flame. A mass of black smoke rose into the clouds. Exploding munitions shot the smoke with dashes of color.

Destruction far away had a strange beauty....

Then the war came to them, the MK-19 of the Rover firing, high-explosive grenades popping, white phosphorous splashing chemical fire at three running figures. In the instant the three died, Lyons saw mismatched fatigues and street clothes. The figures carried Kalashnikov rifles and an RPG launcher. Shrapnel tore their bodies, throwing them back. The searing white points of phosphorous illuminated the rocky ditch where they fell.

Rifles flashed from an orchard wall. As the transport accelerated, Lyons swung the Browning around and hammered the wall, not sighting on the muzzle-flashes, but at the midpoint of the wall. Stone and packed earth flew as the steel-cored slugs broke the wall apart to kill the riflemen crouched behind it.

A rocket launcher sprayed backblast. Lyons saw the RPG warhead end-on as the secondary propellent flashed. But the rocket had been fired too high. The warhead screamed past Lyons as he sighted the Browning and answered the rocketman with armor-piercing slugs.

But another rocketman sighted on the huge target of the truck and semitrailer. At a range of less than a hundred meters, he could not miss.

Lyons looked back as the rocket streaked into the trailer.

12

The blast slammed Gadgets back into the sandbag wall. As the explosion rang in his ears, he felt the trailer lurch, and the floor fall out from under him.

Metal scratched against asphalt, a woman screamed, things crashed in the darkness, the trailer fell sideways on the road. As the trailer's aluminum side scraped against the road's asphalt, Gadgets felt himself falling through space, then hit the sandbags again with a thud. A scraping noise seemed an overwhelming assault on his ears.

Then it stopped.

In the silence, Gadgets heard his heart hammering; the hammering became the sound of autoweapons. Slugs hit the trailer. He found the disposable penlight in his pocket.

Be prepared, he thought as he shone the light over the now upended mobile bunker.

"Wizard! We're hit! Help me with Desmarais!"

"No shit? We're hit? Think maybe we ought to get a second opinion? Wow, looks like we're hit. . . ."

Ammunition cases lay against the wall. The heavy Browning machine gun and MK-19 now stood horizontal on their pedestals.

All the stacked weapons and equipment had shifted

to the one wall that had become the floor. In the clutter, Blancanales struggled to disentangle himself from Desmarais.

Gadgets saw the trapdoor to the bunker far above his head. Before, they had entered by stepping under the trailer then climbing up through the floor. Now they had a problem.

Another flashlight came on. By the glow of Blancanales's flashlight, Gadgets freed a shipping trunk. He made steps by stacking the trunk and ammunition boxes under the trapdoor.

Swinging open the trapdoor, he saw falling snow and darkness. A hundred meters away, autoweapons flashed. The diesel cab lay on its side at the roadside. From behind the shelter of the cab, the Shia drivers returned the fire of ambushers.

A rocket streaked from the darkness. The Shias went flat, and the rocket missed the overturned truck by a hand's width.

"Oh, man. This is serious! Pol! You ready to get out of here?"

Pulling out his belt knife, Blancanales cut the plastic handcuffs linking Desmarais's hands together. He pushed her toward the pile of cases. "Up and out, miss."

Desmarais crawled through and fell with a scream. Autofire hit the trailer. Gadgets ducked.

"They got that exit zeroed!"

"Where's your rifle?" Blancanales searched through the tangled gear to assemble his own equipment.

"Forget the popguns! We got artillery...."

Releasing the clamping lever locking the MK-19 to the pedestal, Gadgets jerked the full-auto grenade launcher free. Groaning with the weight, he had to lower it. He disconnected the box of 40mm grenades. With the linked belt of grenades swinging loose, he picked up the launcher and passed it to Blancanales. Blancanales managed to shove the grenade launcher over the edge of the trapdoor and hook it in place with the swivel-tilt assembly. Gadgets untangled the belt of grenades.

"Do it! Hit them!"

Blancanales sighted on a flashing muzzle. Triggering single shots, he put the first grenade into the orchard wall, the next one over the top. Then he walked the blasts of high explosive and white phosphorous along the wall, hitting the top, the trees behind and a gateway.

Visible in the gray light of burning phosphorous was a person with a rocket launcher. Blancanales sighted and held back the trigger. As the backblast flashed, the night exploded around the rocketman.

Then the rocket hit the trailer.

As THE TRANSPORT SLAMMED through the roadside ditch, Lyons kept the Browning pointed at the autofire. Stone and flesh disintegrated where the .50-caliber slugs hit, rifles firing wild, a dying man staggering, other forms running. Behind Lyons, the Shias fired their PKM machine guns at the ambushers.

The driver steered the awkward troop transport through a wide circle and gunned the engine as he regained the asphalt. Lyons saw the Rover already return-

HE'S EXPLOSIVE. HE'S MACK BOLAN... AGAINST ALL ODDS

He learned his deadly skills in Vietnam...then put them to good use by destroying the Mafia in a blazing one-man war. Now **Mack Bolan** ventures further into the cold to take on his deadliest challenge yet— the KGB's worldwide terror machine.

Follow the lone warrior on his exciting new missions...and get ready for more nonstop action from his high-powered combat teams: **Able Team**—Bolan's famous Death Squad—battling urban savagery too brutal and volatile for regular law enforcement. And **Phoenix Force**—five extraordinary warriors handpicked by Bolan to fight the dirtiest antiterrorist wars, blazing into even greater danger.

Fight alongside these three courageous forces for freedom in all-new action-packed novels! Travel to the gloomy depths of the cold Atlantic, the scorching sands of the Sahara, and the desolate Russian plains. You'll feel the pressure and excitement building page after page, with nonstop action that keeps you enthralled until the explosive conclusion!

Now you can have all the new Gold Eagle novels delivered right to your home!

You won't want to miss a single one of these exciting new action-adventures. And you don't have to! Just fill out and mail the card at right, and we'll enter your name in the Gold Eagle home subscription plan. You'll then receive six brand-new action-packed Gold Eagle books every other month, delivered right to your home! You'll get two Mack Bolan novels, one Able Team and one Phoenix Force, plus one book each from two thrilling, new Gold Eagle libraries, **SOBs** and **Track**. In **SOBs** you'll meet the legendary team of mercenary warriors who fight for justice and win. **Track** features a military and weapons genius on a mission to stop a maniac whose dream is everybody's worst nightmare! Only Track stands between us and nuclear hell!

FREE! The New War Book and Mack Bolan bumper sticker.

As soon as we receive your card we'll rush you the long-awaited New War Book and Mack Bolan bumper sticker—both ABSOLUTELY FREE with your first six Gold Eagle novels.

The New War Book is *packed* with exciting information for Bolan fans: a revealing look at the hero's life...two new short stories...book character biographies...even a combat catalog describing weapons used in the novels! The New War Book is a special collector's item you'll want to read again and again. And it's yours FREE when you mail your card!

Of course, you're under no obligation to buy anything. Your first six books come on a 10-day free trial—if you're not thrilled with them, just return them and owe nothing. The New War Book and bumper sticker are yours to keep, FREE!

Don't miss a single one of these thrilling novels...mail the card now, while you're thinking about it.

HE'S UNSTOPPABLE. AND HE'LL FIGHT TO DEFEND FREEDOM!

FREE! THE NEW WAR BOOK AND MACK BOLAN BUMPER STICKER
when you join our home subscription plan.

Gold Eagle Reader Service, a Division of Worldwide Library
2504 West Southern Avenue, Tempe, Arizona 85282

YES, rush me my FREE New War Book and Mack Bolan bumper sticker and my first six Gold Eagle novels. These first seven books are mine to examine free for 10 days and owe nothing. If I decide to keep these novels, I will pay just $1.95 per book (total $11.70). I will then receive the six Gold Eagle novels every other month, and will be billed the same low price of $11.70 per shipment. I understand that each shipment will contain two Mack Bolan novels, and one each from the Able Team, Phoenix Force, SOBs and Track libraries. There are no shipping and handling or any other hidden charges. I may cancel this arrangement at any time, and The New War Book and bumper sticker are mine to keep as gifts, even if I do not buy any additional books.

166 CIM PAF8

Name	(please print)	
Address		Apt. No.
City	State	Zip
Signature	(If under 18, parent or guardian must sign.)	

This offer limited to one order per household. We reserve the right to exercise discretion in granting membership.

PRINTED IN U.S.A.

ing to the killzone where the overturned truck and semi-trailer lay in the road. Holding down the firing button of the Browning, Lyons provided cover for Powell by raking the length of the orchard wall.

Using the maneuverability of the Land Rover, the Shia driver swerved under the line of .50-caliber tracers.

Powell heard a sound like jet engines as the .50-caliber slugs passed an arm's reach above his head. He reflexively dropped to a crouch.

"Crazy Shia! Cool it—I'm no martyr man!"

The driver whipped through an orchard gate and sped along the other side of the wall sheltering the fanatics of the Muslim Brotherhood. Powell fired straight ahead as the Rover caught the line of militia-men and Syrian deserters in its headlights.

The fanatics spun from the wall and died as they raised their Kalashnikovs, Powell using the full-auto grenade launcher to its maximum lethal effect.

Flashing through clouds of choking acetate smoke and the fumes of phosphorous, Powell rode the buck-ing Land Rover like a stand-up rodeo star. He never released the grips of the MK-19. The Rover hit wounded and dead militiamen, the small vehicle going airborne, crashing back. A slug zipped past Powell as the Rover passed the last ambusher.

From the transport, Lyons watched Powell's wild counterattack and held his fire. Now no rifle fire came from the wall or the orchard. The strange gray light of phosphorous illuminated the length of the wall. Burn-ing wounded screamed and pleaded.

Flames rose from the trailer. On its side, it had been

hit twice, one blast tearing off the back wheels, the other scattering boxes of contraband everywhere.

A man ran from the wrecked diesel truck and fired into a ditch. The headlights of the troop transport revealed one of the Shia drivers finishing off a Syrian deserter. Another Shia waved from the shelter of the overturned cab.

Lyons did not see his partners.

As the transport braked to a stop, Lyons leaped off the tailgate. He looked for the trapdoor of the mobile bunker. He found the open rectangle. Below the trapdoor, he saw an MK-19 grenade launcher without the tripod.

"Wizard! Politician!"

"You okay?" Blancanales called.

"Yeah! What about you?"

"*Alllll* shook up," Gadgets jived. "Get that truck backed up here. We got luggage to offload. Where's that crazy Commie bitch? Tell me she's dead."

"I don't have her!" Lyons shouted back. "She was in there."

"She was. El Señor Politico played the gentleman and boosted her out. You see her?"

"No!" Lyons ran to Hussein and told him to back up the transport. As the others transferred gear from the wrecked trailer, Lyons searched the area for Desmarais.

Beyond the orchard wall, the Rover cruised, still searching for ambushers. All firing had stopped. But Lyons moved cautiously, knowing any number of riflemen could still be watching.

He rushed to the blast-twisted trailer. Shielded by the wheels and open doors, he searched for Desmarais.

He waved a flashlight over the wheels. Not there. Edging around the door, he checked in the spilled boxes of the contraband. The rocket had hit the rear of the trailer, the blast shredding the contraband and blowing out the cargo doors, which had twisted on their hinges. Boxes of toothpaste and breakfast cereal littered the road.

But no Desmarais.

Inside the trailer, a fire had ravaged everything. She could not hide there. He glanced at the roof and saw only the gaping hole where the armor-smashing warhead had torn the aluminum like paper. Flames and smoke poured from the ragged hole.

Sitting on a box, his back to the trailer to minimize his exposure, Lyons swept the road with the light. The sliding trailer had scraped much of the asphalt clean of snow and ice. But near the shoulder, Lyons saw shoe prints, a woman's size. The trail disappeared into the gray distance.

In those street shoes, with only her coat for shelter from the storm, Desmarais would not live long. If she did not freeze to death, she faced a long walk through a war. A young, attractive foreign woman walking among thousands of desperate soldiers, at the mercy of Syrians and Libyans and Palestinians and Soviets— who could say what her chances were?

The others heard Lyons laughing as he returned.

"What's so funny?" Gadgets asked.

"She escaped."

RUNNING THROUGH THE FALLING SNOW, she heard the distant firing stop. She hoped the Arab nationalist force had annihilated the Americans and their mercenaries, but she could not put her freedom at risk. She continued running, glancing back every few seconds.

The Puerto Rican one was the smooth-talking death-squad goon who fought for the fascist monsters holding his island nation in peonage. Whatever his name was, the Puerto Rican one had pushed her through the trap-door, and afterward, she had crawled to a ditch, lain in the snow and watched the fight. As the Americans fired grenades, desperate to forestall their inevitable defeat, she had crawled out of the cross fire.

Then a rocket had streaked over her to deliver a second devastating blast to the Americans. She paused in her crawl, waiting for more fire from the goons in the trailer. But no fire came. Evidently the rocket had killed them.

Hundreds of meters away, the other truck and the Land Rover turned. As they fired, she laughed over the deaths of the two goons in the trailer. She climbed from the ditch and ran on the road, leaving the dead Americans far behind.

But she still had the other two Americans—Powell and that other goon, the blond Nazi—to fear. If they caught her, she could expect only death.

She ran through a pink semidarkness. Ahead of her, red light glowed from the overhanging clouds. She glanced at her watch and saw that four hours remained until morning. The false dawn cast a diffuse pink light on the swirling snow, the glistening road, the forlorn orchards. The pink light allowed her to maintain an easy run.

The highway met a side road. Studying the snow and ice on the asphalt, she saw the recent tire tracks of several vehicles. The last tires to turn here had been double truck tires like those of a cargo trailer. She remembered the truck slowing to turn.

Seeing no lights on the other road, she continued along the highway. She watched for farmhouses or villages. Seeing one house, she approached the door only to see the broken windows and the soot marks. The house had been burned; only the stone walls remained. She continued toward the distant fires.

Rows of headlights appeared: a convoy. She ran to the center of the road and waved. The first pair of lights veered to the side. A covered scout car stopped beside her.

As the convoy continued, Syrian soldiers pointed Kalashnikov rifles at her. She put up her hands and repeated "Journalist" in Arabic and French as they searched her for weapons. They found only her camera. The officer in charge questioned her.

"What are you doing here? Show me your papers."

"Here—documents issued by your government. My name is Anne Desmarais. I am a journalist from Canada. I—"

"Anne Desmarais!" The officer reached into the car for a radio microphone. He spoke fluidly in what Desmarais recognized as Russian.

"Are you looking for me?"

"Not us. Them. . . ." The officer nodded toward the taillights of the convoy.

One of the trucks slowed, then wheeled through a wide turn.

"Who are they?"

The Syrian did not answer.

As the truck braked to a stop, the cab door flew open and Zhgenti stepped out. He held his Uzi.

"My wandering Canadian," he said in his Russian-accented French. He raised the Uzi submachine gun. "How wonderful to see you again. Step away from the officer, please."

"No! I found them! I found them! The Americans. I thought you were all dead. I saw the van burning, but I found the Americans. Don't shoot!"

"Are you lying? It would be better for you to die quickly now than to anger me again."

"No! They are there." She pointed. "I found them, but they captured me. Then someone ambushed them and I escaped and I stopped this car to report the Americans. Two of them may be dead. They are wearing Syrian and Soviet uniforms and using Syrian cars and trucks."

"Soviet uniforms?" Zhgenti set the Uzi's safety. Grabbing Desmarais's arm, he dragged her to the cab of the truck. "We will see...."

"Who are these Syrians?" she asked as they accelerated away.

"It is unimportant. They are convenient. They also hate Americans. Did you... have fun with the Americans?"

"No!"

Zhgenti leered. "Tell me the truth. You persuaded them to let you go, yes?"

The overturned and burning trailer appeared. "No! There! See? There was an ambush. That's how I escaped."

After an inspection of the wrecked truck and trailer, Zhgenti returned to Desmarais. "You have saved your life. Now we must pursue the Americans. What did they tell you? Where are they going?"

She remembered what the Shia militiaman had told her. "Damascus. This way, this road was only a detour, because of fighting somewhere else."

Nodding, Zhgenti studied a map. "Damascus... I do not believe their goal is Damascus. There must be somewhere else they intend—"

"They may be searching for a group of Iranians who are making rockets. Somewhere in the Bekaa, Iranian Revolutionary Guards are making rockets to attack America. Perhaps the place is on the road to Damascus. Look at your map. If they were going anywhere else, they would have gone north or south on these other highways. But they did not."

"Oh, yes... and there is only one road to Damascus. Good. I will have the Syrians radio ahead for their soldiers to watch for these Americans in Soviet uniforms. The roadblocks will stop them. There is no doubt we will find them."

The convoy of Syrian troop transports moved through the night, pursuing Able Team.

13

"High tech this ain't," Gadgets muttered as he pounded nails with a wrench, snow and a 100 KPH wind numbing his hands.

In the back of the troop transport, Gadgets nailed the tripod of an MK-19 full-auto grenade launcher to the plank deck of the truck. Americans and Shia militiamen crowded the back of the transport. Stacked boxes and cases of ammunition stood against the slatted sides.

The American and Shia crew had emptied the gear and ammunition from the wrecked trailer. The Browning .50-caliber machine gun had been damaged so they had left it in the trailer to burn. But they had salvaged the MK-19 and its tripod.

They had also salvaged contraband. Placed on top of the ammunition cases, the boxes of designer jeans and toothpaste and cheap electronics concealed the U.S. Army codes stenciled on the green ammunition cases.

As the two Syrian army vehicles continued east, the American electronics specialist secured the MK-19 tripod. He pounded the nails into the planks, then bent them over the feet of the tripod. To test his work, he kicked the tripod. Two legs held, but one broke free.

"Where's my power drill? Where's my electric wrench?" Gadgets clutched at the collar of his Soviet coat. "Where's my electric blanket?"

"Calm down, Wizard," Blancanales told him. Watching the desolate winter landscape of fields and rocky foothills, he held his M-16/M-203 ready, the ripple grip of the grenade launcher braced on the top side slat. "All we got to do is hit those Iranians, and we're on our way back."

"Got to find them, got to study them, then we hit them, then we get to split this winter wonderland."

"Weren't we in the Caribbean just a few days ago, riding the surf?"

"Oh, yeah, and now it's a skiing adventure. Give me that box—that one."

"The jeans?"

"Yeah, that one."

Blancanales watched as his partner hacked open the box with a K-bar knife, then cut a pair of jeans into strips.

Gadgets used the strips to lash the legs of the tripod to the nails. Then he jerked the heavy MK-19 across the truck and mounted it on the tripod. The full-auto grenade launcher now pointed behind the truck. Gadgets sat behind it and swiveled it, sighting on the storm clouds, then on a distant hilltop.

He fired a single grenade. After a few seconds, they saw a pinpoint flash.

"Save the ammunition, Wizard," Lyons called from his post near the Browning. Wrapped in blankets, he sat between boxes. Only his eyes showed between his Soviet fur hat and scarf. "I think we'll need it."

"I pronounce this weapon in working order. Anyone chases us, they got very serious problems. No doubt about it."

Blancanales pointed ahead. "Another traffic jam."

Gadgets and Lyons stood and looked. A few kilometers ahead, a long line of taillights curved through the darkness. The diffused glare of headlights illuminated a pass through the foothills.

Beyond the pass, the clouds flashed with the reflected light of high explosive. Soviet artillery rockets streaked through the air, arching in several directions as forces exchanged barrages.

The Rover point car slowed and their hand-radios buzzed.

"We're not going that way," Powell told them.

"Second the motion," Gadgets answered.

"There's a road that might lead to the village," Powell told them. "But it'll be rough. Coming up."

After another kilometer, the Rover led the troop transport off the highway. They lurched and swayed along a dirt track of frozen ruts. Holes and jutting rocks slammed the transport from side to side. The dirt road led higher into the foothills.

They came to the ridge. Below them stretched a panorama of war.

Shellfire lit the hills. Streaking rockets splashed fire on targets. Intermittently, tracers streaked down from jet aircraft that remained unseen in the night sky.

A sound like prolonged distant thunder came to them.

"Somebody tell me that I don't have to go down there," Gadgets wished out loud.

"Not only are you going down there," Powell said as he high-stepped through the snow, "but you're walking down there. We can't risk headlights. So one of us walks ahead with a flashlight."

ZHGENTI CURSED IN RUSSIAN as he and Desmarais returned to the convoy of Syrian troop transports. They had inspected all the vehicles in the long line of waiting trucks and tanks and troop transports. Desmarais had not seen the Americans.

Nor had the Americans in Soviet uniforms attempted to pass the roadblock. Desmarais had described them and their two remaining vehicles in detail. The Syrian officers repeated that they had not allowed the Americans to pass.

By long-distance radio, Zhgenti then spoke with a KGB superior in the Soviet embassy. The officer noted the information and assured Zhgenti that the Syrians would dispatch helicopters to search for the two vehicles. But in the confusion and wreckage of the insurrection. . . .

"Excuses!" Zhgenti kicked rocks. "They send me to Beirut to kill Americans and the Americans are already gone. I come into this mishmash to kill Americans, and the Americans hide in Soviet uniforms. I get their descriptions and have the Syrians block the roads and the Americans disappear. I call for assistance and they tell me it will be difficult. Difficult! Of course it is difficult; the Americans are paid to make it difficult; they use all their wits to make it difficult!"

"If you cannot find them in Lebanon," Desmarais

suggested, "perhaps you could wait for them in Damascus."

"I don't believe they will go there. Security is too tight. They must pass too many document checks. To leave Lebanon, they will go out through Beirut."

"But the Shia said Damascus."

"So? You should know that lies are cheap."

"But he had no reason to lie. And my question surprised him. Sometimes people tell the truth when surprised."

"Do you?"

"The Americans know the Syrians and the Iranians worked together on this. Perhaps they want to attack the Iranians. It would be possible to station men outside the Iranian embassy, would it not?"

"Yes, possible. But the Americans will not go there!"

"It is possible. And where else will you look? Out there?" Desmarais swept the night with an arm. "They could be anywhere. Even with helicopters, how could you find them? I tell you, those fascist goons calculate what is impossible and then do it. I say continue the search, post men in Beirut to watch, but also post men in Damascus. The Americans will do what you do not expect, that is certain."

"True." Zhgenti waved away clouds of diesel smoke as they passed an idling truck. "Canadian, I am glad I let you live. You are sometimes useful. But do not try my patience again."

ARTILLERY SHELLS SCREAMED DOWN, high explosives momentarily lighting the snow-covered hills.

But without effect. The shells struck nothing, but broke rocks and pitted the snow. Twice Powell had called for halts. With the engines off, no one speaking or moving, they had listened for other forces in the area. They had heard nothing—no clanking tanks, no trucks, no rifles—only the continuing explosions of the untargeted artillery fire.

"Think they know we're out here," Gadgets wondered, "but they just don't know where?"

They heard the crunch of boots in snow. Lyons returned to the transport and passed the flashlight to Gadgets. "Your turn. Stay cool."

"Oh, yeah, man. Supercool. Walk point in the dark with a flashlight."

Wrapping a blanket around his shoulders, Gadgets jumped into the snow, snapped on the flashlight and preceded the Rover.

A handkerchief over the glass reduced the beam to a soft white glow. Walking fast, Gadgets held his hand over the top of the light as he waved the flashlight back and forth over the road. The Rover and Mercedes troop transport advanced behind him.

"There are no mines under this snow," Gadgets said to himself. "There are no Arab legions waiting to ambush me. There are no artillery spotters working this territory. I'm out here all by myself. Alone in the snow."

A light winked. Gadgets dropped. "No, I ain't...I ain't alone."

The Rover and truck stopped. Gadgets saw the light reappear over the curve of a low hill. He whispered to Powell, "We got something up ahead."

Gadgets heard his hand-radio clicking. "On my way, Wizard," Lyons told him. Seconds later, fur-hatted, his Atchisson-modelled Konzak assault shotgun in his hands, Lyons crouched beside Gadgets. "Where?"

"There."

Without speaking, they moved off the road and cut up the slope of the hill. Far in the distance, three shells exploded. A flare burst into searing light, illuminating a hilltop. More shells resounded. Lyons and Gadgets continued, using the faint light to avoid rocks.

At the crest, the distant flare light revealed another road. The road wove across the gray landscape to what appeared to be a sandbag bunker. A light came from inside.

Beyond the bunker, they saw three distinct sets of perimeter lights on three lines of chain link and concertina circling a cluster of buildings.

"We have arrived," Gadgets said into his hand-radio.

"The village?" Powell asked.

"Anyplace else around here got three concentric perimeters? And bunkers and all that?"

"There's a checkpoint on the road," Lyons said into his own radio. "Sandbagged. No one outside. Got to take them before we can go past."

"I'll send up Akbar and Politician."

Lyons looked at the Konzak he carried. "Nah, bring up the trucks. They won't see them and I want to change gear."

They jogged back through the snow to the road. Two minutes later, the Rover and the Mercedes, without headlights, in low gear, silently pulled up.

"This is it, right?" Blancanales handed Lyons the American-made Kalashnikov and the bandolier of magazines.

"Yeah, we might have to walk in, and this Konzak's a giveaway."

"What about my over-and-under?" Blancanales slapped the black ripple grip of his M-16/M-203.

"The Konzak doesn't shoot high-ex forty. Just keep that out of sight. Who knows what'll happen down there?"

"I got an idea what'll happen," Gadgets answered.

"Then let's go do it to them." Lyons cinched up his bandolier of ComBloc mags and led the line of men across the snow. Akbar jogged alongside Gadgets.

"So what's the scam, man? You hotshots got a plan?"

"Where'd you learn to talk that jive, foreigner?" Gadgets asked.

"In da bunkers. Me and Powell. And some spade Marines. Nothing but shit screaming down out of the sky—boom, boom, ka-boom. Lotsa time to talk, I tell you. I taught them the poetry of the Koran, they taught me to speak American."

"Quiet!" Lyons snarled.

They filed down the slope to the road. A kilometer away, shells burst in the lighted village, a building collapsing in a ball of dust. In a seemingly random pattern, other shells hit within the perimeters, in the open fields, and on the mountain slopes kilometers away.

The flashes of light illuminated the hillside, and the four men descended quickly. Lyons stopped at the road and noticed the smooth surface of snow.

"Nothing in or out tonight," he whispered to Blancanales.

"They have helicopters."

"Yeah, but the rockets won't travel by helicopter. And I don't see an airfield here."

"True."

Easing down into a roadside ditch, Lyons found himself standing on ice. He led the others toward the Syrian bunker. Their boots slipped on the frozen mud and ice, and sometimes the ice cracked under their weight. Lyons cautioned them with a hiss as they neared the Syrians.

A shell landed a hundred meters away. They went flat in the ditch, their ears ringing with the one explosion as they waited for others. Bits of ice and rocks fell. Then silence.

Then voices came from the checkpoint's bunker. Akbar provided a whispered summary: "One of them thinks it's the Israelis. Another says it can't be, because no one's been hit. Yet another is complaining because they should have left already."

"What? Should have left already?"

"Yes, that is what they say."

Lyons slung his weapon across his back. Taking out his modified-for-silence Colt, he eased back the slide to chamber the first .45 hollowpoint from the 10-round extended magazine.

"I go first. Wizard, back me up with your Beretta. We got to move quick."

And he moved, silently moving from the ditch to the bunker.

As Gadgets followed, he felt his hand-radio buzz. But he did not stop.

Behind him in the ditch, Blancanales pressed his transmit key and whispered, "What goes on?"

Powell spoke quickly. "A car or truck is coming. Don't get caught in the open."

Looking across the snow and ruts of the road, Blancanales saw his partners standing against the dark sandbags of the bunker, utterly exposed.

14

Colonel Dastgerdi went from office to office on a final tour of inspection. His electric lantern illuminated the empty rooms and crated equipment where his technicians had assembled and tested his designs. At any moment the shelling would stop and the call would come announcing the elimination of the rebellious factions. And the trucks would depart, the technicians and workers and soldiers for Damascus, the rockets for the Lebanese seaport of Tripoli.

Only the empty rooms and the echoing underground factory would remain. Dastgerdi had already arranged for the Islamic Amal militia to take the village as a base and weapons depot. After the terror rocketing of the inauguration of the President of the United States, the Islamic Amal would suffer the first counterstrikes by American forces. Then as the momentum of strike and counterstrike accelerated, as the Americans discovered the innumerable details linking Iran and Syria to the assassination of their President and hundreds of officials and spectators, the war would cross the borders into Syria and on to Iran as the revenge-blinded Americans attacked the nations they believed responsible.

Shining his battery light on an office wall, Dastgerdi

saw a poster of the scowling Ayatollah Khomeini. Cemented in place with plastic, then painted repeatedly with clear plastic, the poster was there to stay. The face of Khomeini, along with the cut-out newspaper photos of the terror bombing of the Marine Peacekeeping Headquarters in Beirut, had become part of the wall.

The Farsi scrawl that translated as "Death to America" had also been painted over with plastic.

If American commandos invaded this place, they would see what they expected. Dastgerdi had ordered posters and photos and slogans to be displayed on all the walls of the village. If the Americans brought video cameras, the world would see.

So much planning and work. . . .

Dastgerdi descended the steel spiral staircase to the underground factory, heard the noise of tools and the voices of all his personnel. Everyone was waiting for the trucks to leave.

The call would come any minute. . . .

STEADYING HIMSELF against the wall of sandbags, Lyons looked through the firing slot and into the muzzle of a 12.7mm Degtyarev machine gun. But the weapon was unmanned.

The Syrians stood around a fire, arguing and gesturing, warming their hands. One man searched a crumpled carton for a last cigarette and found nothing. Cursing, he threw the wadded pack into the fire.

They wore blankets over their coats. The blankets covered their Kalashnikov rifles.

Under his coat, Lyons felt the buzzer of his hand-radio. Gadgets nudged him. Easing away from the firing slot, Lyons reached into his coat for his radio. Gadgets shook his head and passed him an earphone. Lyons plugged it into his ear. Gadgets clicked the transmit key.

"You got a truck coming—" Blancanales started.

"No," Powell interrupted. "It's a Zil limo."

Lyons chanced a whisper. "How far?"

"Two kilometers maybe. Going slow."

"Move it," Lyons told them. "We'll take that limo into the base."

Lyons snapped down the left-hand grip lever of his Colt. Lyons pointed to himself and then at the bunker. Gadgets nodded.

Lyons crept under the machine-gun slot, then stood. He brushed off his Soviet coat and pulled his AK around so that the automatic rifle crossed his gut. He pat-checked his Colt's extra 10-round magazine in his coat pocket. Taking a deep breath of the frigid air, he walked into the bunker, the Colt held down against his coat, his thumb on the safety-fire selector.

The Syrians were startled; one soldier snapped a salute. Lyons brought up the Colt smoothly, his left hand taking the lever midway in the arch, his left thumb locking into the oversize trigger guard and his right thumb sweeping down the fire selector two clicks.

A 3-shot burst hit the saluting Syrian in the face, the hollowpoint slugs exploding through his skull, bone and blood, and fingers spraying the other soldiers. Lyons continued forward, pointing the pistol at the staring eyes and gaping mouth of another soldier. A 3-shot burst took his head off above the jaw.

A third Syrian finally reacted, throwing aside his

blanket, reaching for the pistol-grip of a Kalashnikov. Lyons continued forward, his left leg snapping a kick to the groin of his opponent. Gasping, the soldier fell, his hand trying to find his rifle. Lyons fired down into the top of the man's head.

Pivoting, his arms straightened, he fired the last .45-caliber slug at the last Syrian as the panicking soldier grabbed for his rifle. The slug snapped the Syrian's head sideways, gouging a bloody track from his left cheek through his ear.

The slide of the Colt locked back. His gashed face contorting with a scream of panic and rage, the Syrian swung his Kalashnikov around.

A burst of three subsonic 9mm slugs took out his left eye. Another burst punched into his temple. Lyons drove a kick into the rifle in the Syrian's hands, and Gadgets stepped close and fired a point-blank burst from his Beretta through the Syrian's forehead.

"Die already!"

Ejecting the empty mag from his Colt, Lyons pocketed it and jammed in another 10-round magazine. Gadgets put the suppressor of his Beretta against the necks of the two Syrians who still had heads and fired bursts of 9mm slugs into their brain stems.

Lyons took out his hand-radio. "Politician. You watch the road. Send Akbar over here. He'll play Syrian when that limo comes."

"He's on his way. Anything goes wrong, get down."

"Don't hit the limo."

Akbar entered. "Hey, cowboys! What's going—" He saw the sprawled corpses. The sight of the open skulls and blood-glistening walls stopped his jive. He kept his sight off the floor when he spoke, his voice suddenly cool and professional. "What must I do?"

"Where's the limo?" Lyons asked. "How close?"

"Some minutes. It goes slowly on the road."

"You'll take the place of the guard out there. Stop them and check their papers. Call out for your Soviet advisor to check the passengers in the back. We need the doors open. They must open the doors. We don't want to mess up the windows, understand? The limousine must look perfect when it goes to the next checkpoint."

"I understand." Carefully avoiding looking at their ruined heads, Akbar compared his Syrian uniform to the uniforms worn by the dead guards. He took a blanket from the floor and draped it over his shoulders before stepping into the snow.

Lyons spoke into his hand-radio. "Marine, this is the Ironman."

"Receiving. The limo's close now."

"Get the truck and your car moving. I want you to move up to this position and park. You'll wait here while we go in. I want you close in case we need backup."

"You're going in?"

"Company instructions. Isn't good enough to ex them out. Got to study the situation, take back information for the clerks—"

Gadgets interrupted. "I can't go in until the truck gets here. I need my bag of tricks."

"No problem. Wizard tells me we wait until the truck gets here. He needs his equipment."

"Check."

Lyons pocketed the radio. He and Gadgets crouched behind the machine gun. Through the firing slot, they watched the Soviet staff car approach.

The Zil limousine, a long black behemoth with the styling of a 1950 Checker, rattled and banged over the frozen road. The flags of the Union of Soviet Socialist Republics and the Syrian Arab Republic hung sodden on fender antennae. Wire in the edges of the flags maintained the rectangular shapes.

Akbar strode into the road and waved a flashlight. He put up a hand to halt the limousine. Worn-out brakes squealed as the Zil shuddered to a stop. Akbar went to the driver's window.

"Stand by for our cue." Lyons stood in the doorway of the bunker and straightened his Soviet uniform. He checked his loaded and locked Colt. Keeping the oversize government Model against his Soviet-army coat, he watched Akbar shine the flashlight into the interior of the Zil.

Flashes of white light lit the foothills, the booms of exploding artillery shells coming an instant later. Akbar argued with the driver. The driver's arm waved a handful of documents. Akbar called out to the bunker. He motioned for his Soviet advisor to personally check the identification of the dignitaries.

His collar up over his face, his Russian fur hat pulled down to his eyes, Lyons strode to the limousine. He ignored the papers in the hand of the Syrian driver and knocked on the window of the back door with his left hand.

The driver shouted at Lyons in Arabic. His back to

the driver, Lyons ignored the Arabic and then the phrases of Russian. He kept knocking on the back window, his body turned slightly to hide the suppressed Colt in his right hand.

Voices snarled Russian invective as the back door swung open. Lyons leaned into the Zil's warmth and saw two squat, scowl-faced Soviets, one in the gray coat and suit of a diplomat, the other in the green wool of the Soviet army. The Soviet in the army coat had an insignia on his coat collar of a triangle of three stars over two red stripes: a colonel.

The first .45 hollowpoint punched through his sneering lips, smashing through his teeth and upper palate to explode through his brain. Lyons flicked down his Colt's fire selector and fired a 3-shot burst through the upraised hands of the diplomat, the slugs tearing away fingers and continuing into the elegant gray overcoat. Throwing the falling Soviet colonel aside, Lyons confirmed the blood fountaining from the chest of the diplomat.

Akbar jerked the driver out the open window, the window frame pinning the Syrian's hands as he struggled for the pistol at his belt. Working together, Akbar and Lyons dragged the driver out of the car. But he twisted out of their grip and snatched the pistol from his holster. Gadgets and Lyons fired at the driver simultaneously, .45 hollowpoints and steel-cored subsonic 9mm slugs slapping into his chest and face, a second burst of full-powered .45 slugs ripping away his face and jaw, spilling his brains into the snow.

Blancanales jogged from the ditch. The four men

worked quickly, pulling the bodies from the limousine, wiping blood from the interior.

"Think the Agency would want their papers and identification?" Lyons asked his partners.

"Perhaps we don't want them to know what we're doing," Blancanales commented. "That one's a colonel. The other one could be an ambassador. Perhaps this will lead to a diplomatic crisis."

"Oh, no!" Gadgets faked fear. "Think the Agency would stop sending us out to do their shitwork?"

Lyons laughed. "I'll bag up all the documents. Wizard—" Lyons pointed to the approaching Land Rover and troop transport truck.

Finding a briefcase in the limo, Lyons stripped the dead Soviets of identification. He emptied their pockets into the briefcase, taking their handwritten notes, their wallets and appointment books, even their keys and coins. He took the gold-stars-and-red-stripes insignia off the colonel's coat collar and fitted the insignia onto his own coat.

"What a low-life," Powell commented as he approached. "Stealing from the dead."

Lyons ignored the jive. "Get some of your men to drag these somewhere. There's four more inside the bunker. Before they cover up the bodies, I want them to use grenades to blow off the hands and faces of these Soviets. I don't want them ever identified."

"Comprendo totolo," Powell answered in Texmex, then continued in English. "Let the Commies have some missing in action." He switched to Arabic and issued instructions to his Shia militiamen allies. They dragged the bloody corpses over the hill.

Gadgets jumped off the back of the transport with a heavy canvas bag in each hand.

"You ready to go in?" Lyons asked.

Artillery shells exploded less than a kilometer away. The men flinched. Gadgets shook his head. "I'm never ready for this, but I got my kit together so let's go so we can get out of this shit."

"Any Cubans operate with the Soviets?" Blancanales asked Powell.

"In Syria? Never heard any Spanish, but that doesn't mean anything."

"Then I'm a Cuban."

"In the limo," Lyons told his partners. He turned to Akbar, but he did not need to speak.

"You Americans are crazy." The young Shia took the driver's seat. He set the dead Syrian's transit documents on the dash above the steering wheel. Blancanales took the passenger-side front seat.

As he got into the back, Lyons called to Powell. "It might happen fast. Be ready to move when we come out."

"Yes, Colonel Ironmannokski." Powell gave him a mock salute. "If you come out...."

15

A white flash, then a concussion came as a shell exploded along the wire surrounding the village. Rocks clanged on the Zil. Akbar switched on a radio mounted under the dashboard and spun through channels of static.

Two hundred meters ahead was the outer gate, a squat bunker and watchtower providing security for the entrance. Lights on poles flooded the gates with day-bright glare. But no soldiers stood guard. No soldiers moved in the watchtower.

Rockets screamed overhead. All four men looked up, as if they could see the fire arcs of the rockets through the Zil's roof. Seconds later, they heard the distant explosions.

"It's jobs like this," Gadgets commented quietly, "that make me think about quitting government work. Sometimes it's just too, too much."

No one else spoke. Akbar guided the Zil through the ruts and drifting snow. The headlights revealed the sandbags and heavy machine guns of the bunker. But no soldiers.

Akbar stopped at the gate. No challenging voice came from the bunker. They waited. Akbar rolled down his window and called in Arabic.

No one came out. Lyons rolled down his window. He saw no one. Then he leaned over the front seat and pressed on the horn. Only Gadgets spoke. "Too weird."

Soldiers appeared. Wrapped in blankets, flashlights in their hands, they looked at the Soviet limousine. Lyons rolled up his window as Akbar motioned the soldiers over to check his documents.

One soldier dashed to the window, held a flashlight on the signatures and stamps of the documents, then waved the light over the faces of the passengers. Starting to the gate, he shouted.

Another soldier appeared. They rolled the gate open and waved the limo through. As Akbar shifted, a roar crossed the sky. Voices were raised. The soldiers ran for the bunker, leaving the gate open. The roar faded into the distance.

"A jet," Akbar told the others. "They said, 'Israeli jet' and ran away."

"Was it Israeli?" Blancanales asked.

Akbar pointed to the lighted fences, the lighted watchtowers, the lights coming from the low buildings of the village. "This would not still be here."

"It does look like a neon bull's-eye," Gadgets added. "There's no way they could—"

"Quit the speculation," Lyons interrupted. "We're through the first gate—"

"And the second." Akbar pointed. "It is open."

The gate in the second fence, in the center of the minefields, stood open. Akbar accelerated, speeding over the hundred meters of gravel and snow to the inner gate. No soldiers manned the positions at the entry to the village.

An orange-white flash erupted from the frozen earth of the minefield, the scream of the artillery shell simultaneous with the explosion. Lyons looked back and saw dirt and stone falling everywhere around the smoking crater. Other explosions popped as the falling debris triggered antipersonnel mines.

As Blancanales pointed out directions, Akbar wove through the narrow streets of the village. He circled a block of collapsing stone houses, then stopped.

Blancanales oriented his partners. "That way and to the left is the gate. The ramps to what the Agency analysts think is an underground structure is to the right and down two long blocks. There's several houses and shops that are used for administration and technical workshops all along the street."

"Take this—" Gadgets passed one of his canvas bags to Lyons "—and don't drop it."

"You got enough in here to blow this place away?"

"No way. Just minitransmitters and recorders. And radio-pops and det-cord and a kilo or two of plastique."

"Then how are you going to do it?"

"Use your head," Gadgets answered. "Solid-fuel rockets. High-explosive warheads. Why should I carry in the bang when the bang's already here?"

"Ready to go?" Blancanales asked his partners. "Your equipment ready, Wizard?"

Lyons and Gadgets answered by stepping into the blowing snow. Standing in the dark and narrow street, they listened. The distant rumbling of artillery continued. But in the village—the abandoned houses, the shell-shattered shops—they heard nothing: no voices, no movement.

They walked from the limousine. Playing the role of Soviet officers, they made no effort at concealment, walking in the center of the narrow street. Lyons continued to the corner and then stood and looked in all directions, scanning the wide central street for Syrians. Akbar stopped beside him.

"If we run into Syrians," Lyons told the Shia, "we'll just walk past. Unless they're alone, or unless they look like the commander, then we take them, put questions to them."

"Just act natural," Gadgets added. "We're Soviets, we own the place."

Akbar shook his head. "Americans, crazy...."

They turned right, passing boarded-over doorways and windows. Walls of sandbags blocked narrow passages between collapsing buildings. Other than flapping sheets of plastic, nothing moved.

A hundred meters away were lights over a retaining wall of cast concrete, which satellite photos and prisoner information identified as part of a ramp leading to an underground complex. But neither the satellite nor the prisoners had provided information on the interior. Rouhani, the leader of the Iranian Revolutionary Guards captured in Mexico, did not have the intelligence or memory to sketch the complex. And the Syrian official, Choufi, captured in Nicaragua, had never actually entered the underground area.

Lyons spotted footsteps, imprinted on the recent snow, leading from the street to a doorway. Signaling the others to stop, he handed the canvas bag of explosives to Gadgets, who passed both bags to Akbar.

Then Lyons slipped out his silenced Colt and went to the door to listen. He heard only silence inside. Pressing his back against the stone wall, he exposed one hand as he worked the latch lever.

The door opened. Warm air blew past his face. Lyons waited, listening. An arm's distance to his side, Gadgets and Blancanales watched the street. When Lyons moved, Gadgets shifted, bringing up his Beretta 93-R to back up his partner.

Lyons crouched beside the door of the dark shop, listening, his eyes sweeping the black interior. He smelled diesel exhaust and machine oil and the stale odor of many men breathing and smoking and sweating. The faint sounds of voices and movement came to him.

A line of gray light glowed across the room. Holding the Colt in his right hand, Lyons felt through his pockets for a flashlight. A beam appeared from behind him. Gadgets swept the interior with the tiny light of a disposable penlight.

Then the other three men stepped silently into the room. Blancanales eased the door shut. The penlight revealed tables and chairs, a recently swept floor, a poster of Khomeini on the wall, and another door on the opposite wall.

"Smell it?" Lyons whispered.

"Like a garage," Blancanales answered.

Crossing the room in two steps, Lyons crouched beside the second door. He put his fingers to the crack between the floor and bottom of the closed door. Nodding, he pointed to the door.

Akbar stayed back, the two canvas bags of explosives in his hands, as Able Team snapped into a routine of long experience: Lyons stood beside the doorway, his back to the stone-and-plaster wall, while Gadgets and Blancanales took positions to provide crisscrossing cover fire. Then Lyons opened the door and rushed through the doorway.

A long concrete corridor, presently unpopulated, stretched before him; obviously, it connected several buildings. Gray light from the ends of the corridor revealed doors on both sides. Handrails indicated stairs leading down. Lyons motioned Gadgets to follow. Blancanales stayed behind to watch their backs.

Silently, Colt in hand, Lyons rushed to the stairs, whose steel-mesh steps descended to a place from which voices and banging emanated.

He tried the knob of the nearest door; the door opened. Using his flashlight, he saw a large workshop. Tables with electrical outlets lined the walls. In the center, patterns in the stained concrete floor indicated places where machines had been bolted to the floor. Posters of the Ayatollah Khomeini glared down from the wall.

The building lurched, and the roar of an explosion overwhelmed Lyons for an instant. Stones rattled and dust trickled down from the walls and ceiling.

Returning to the corridor, he motioned for the others to come. Gadgets relayed the signal to Blancanales and Akbar. While they rushed to the end of the corridor, Gadgets maintained his position, then joined them.

In the workshop, Lyons whispered to his partners, ''That passage leads underground. Sounds like they're working down there. Maybe assembling the transportation for the rockets.''

Gadgets opened a canvas bag and sorted through plastic envelopes by the glow of his penlight. ''The fact is, they ain't up here. That tells me they're probably down there. Hiding out from the war. Getting their show on the road. Thing to do is to go take look-see. And for that, I want to volunteer—'' he grinned and pointed to the young Shia militiaman ''—Akbar.''

''Me? I am not trained to be a secret agent.''

''No problem,'' Gadgets jived. ''Go down, walk around, listen to what the people are talking about, and if you see the main man, stick one of these near enough to monitor what he's saying.'' The Able Team electronics specialist put three thick button-sized minimicrophone-transmitters in the Shia's hand. ''But be cool about it. Go—we'll cover you.''

Not allowing Akbar time to think, Gadgets and Lyons escorted him to the steel steps. Gadgets whispered a last warning as Akbar crept slowly, silently down the stairs.

''Be cool. . . or get cooled.''

Every step down took Akbar farther from the security of the weapons of the Americans. In his home streets, in times of trouble, he had often obeyed orders that placed him at risk—holding a position despite artillery and small-arms fire, or running shipments through the checkpoints of hostile militias, for example. But then his militia, a force equal or superior to the enemies he faced, backed him and provided firepower in case of a reverse or miscalculation. Now he faced the professional, career soldiers of the Syrian army, and its secret police, with only three Americans standing behind him.

But he prepared himself, intellectually at least, and continued his descent. He reached the bottom of the steel steps. No sentries challenged him.

A long, empty passage led to a rectangle of light. Standing beside the last step, Akbar saw through the rectangle Syrians operating forklifts. He waited a moment, listening, then approached the light.

As he walked, he loosened his scarf and unbuttoned his overcoat. Passing a doorway, he glanced inside and saw two soldiers packing small boxes into a wooden crate. They did not look up.

At the end of the passage, he braced himself, then stepped around the corner and into the glare of the fluorescent lights. He saw an underground factory in disarray, as though in the final stage of disassembly.

At the far end, men in civilian coveralls crowded around diesel trucks and trailers. Syrian soldiers stood at troop transports. Everywhere soldiers and technicians worked to dismantle the facility.

Then Akbar saw the commander. The Syrian wore a tailored uniform and a Soviet wool greatcoat, and talked with men in coveralls, his breath clouding. The group referred to blueprints and drawings, then one of the technicians called to some type of assistant, who ran to a trailer and brought back a notebook.

Someone grabbed Akbar. "What are you doing?" A voice demanded.

"Ah...." Panicking, Akbar could say nothing as the hand spun him.

"Nothing! That's what you're doing!" A Syrian

noncom shoved the handles of a moving dolly into his hands. "Take this box to the others. It's tools, hear me? Don't let it get packed in the wrong crate. Move!"

Without speaking, Akbar wrestled the dolly into a roll. Not knowing where to take the wooden box, he aimed for the table of blueprints where the Syrian commander stood with the technicians. As he approached, he slipped his hand into his pocket and removed one of the miniature microphone-transmitters.

The box banged into a workbench; Akbar lost his grip and the dolly slammed down onto the concrete floor. The commander and his staff looked at him, then resumed their conversation.

Squeezing between the blueprint table and the box, Akbar placed a minitransmitter under the table. Then he struggled with the heavy box for a moment. Jerking the dolly back, he wheeled past the commander.

Akbar looked for a place to dump his cargo. Beyond the diesel trucks and trailers, he saw the Mercedes limousine, the doors open, an orderly loading luggage into the trunk. Steering the dolly past the trucks, Akbar swung around to the front of the Mercedes and looked back. A diesel truck blocked the sight of the soldiers at the troop transport. The open trunk lid blocked the sight of the driver.

As he passed the rear door of the limo, Akbar pretended to stumble again, letting the dolly slam down. As he struggled, he tossed a minitransmitter into a compartment in the door of the limousine.

Moving fast, he left the box near the second trailer. Jogging behind the dolly, he wove through the forklifts and worktables to the passage leading up.

The noncom spotted him. "What took you so long? Go in there and take another box."

Akbar saluted. "Sir! My lieutenant ordered me up to the street. To stand guard."

Squinting his sun-weathered eyes, the noncom sneered. "You deserve it, you lazy creature. Go up there! Freeze! Let the Israelis blow you up! Go!"

Akbar ran up the steel stairs.

16

Akbar translated the transmitted voices. "He's talking about 'the signal strength' and 'the terminal-guidance machines.' This is all very technical.... He's telling them not to worry about the transmitters, the transmitters are not their concern, he is sure the transmitters will be in place before the launch of the rockets.... 'The multiple transmissions will not cancel the signals....' He's telling them thanks for their work, they will never receive the recognition they deserve, but they will learn of their success if they watch television in January, then they can rejoice."

In a corner of the abandoned workshop, Gadgets listened to the running translation of the Syrian's farewell address to his group of engineers. His partners watched the doors: Lyons the corridor doorway, Blancanales the door outside. After a few minutes, Akbar shook his head.

"He has moved away from the table. I can only hear noise from the others now. The scientists are gone."

Gadgets checked through a mental list of details. "He said, 'miniature units'?" Akbar nodded. "And 'terminal guidance'? And 'multiple transmitters'? And 'independent agents'?"

Akbar nodded to each question. Gadgets considered

the information as his partners maintained their watch. Outside, the distant thunder of artillery strikes came infrequently. No shells had struck near the base for the previous half-hour. Only the snowstorm continued, gusts of wind blowing subzero air under the street door.

"What's your opinion, Mr. Wizard?" Lyons whispered.

"These crazies have got what the Iranians thought they had. What I mean is, the Iranians thought they had ninety-six Soviet 240mm rockets. Complete with some kind of custom terminal-guidance system. That is, after someone at the approximate target area activates a homing signal, they launch the rockets, then the homing signal gives the rockets something to zero in on. Turned out the Iranians had real rockets with dummy guidance units and phony transmitters. These Syrians have actually got the real thing."

"Why did the Iranians have the dummies?" Blancanales asked.

"A decoy, just like George told us on the plane. The Syrians let the Iranians go in with the phony stuff, they get hit, we think we've closed it down, and then they come in with the big surprise. That's what I think they're thinking. Fooled us. Except the Agency untangled all the phony equipment and compared it to what the Iranians thought they had. Now it's for sure."

"Deception," Lyons commented. "Run us around chasing real crazies with phony rockets—"

A buzz came from their hand-radios. Gadgets answered. "Talk to the Wizard."

"We got another limo coming," Powell reported.

"A limousine?"

"One. No trucks. No escort vehicles. Just a limo. Want us to zap them?"

"Hold on, we'll take a vote." Gadgets turned to his partners. "Can't question dead ones. I got another minimike back in the truck. How about Mr. Marine puts it on them and listens in?"

Lyons and Blancanales nodded agreement. Gadgets spoke to Powell again, directing him to take the miniature transmitter and receiver from his equipment and place the microphone in the limousine.

"Will do, specialist. You'll know when it's transmitting."

"No, I won't. It's on another frequency than the ones I have here. You've got to monitor. So go, get to it."

The voice of Dastgerdi came from the receiver's tiny speaker. Akbar summarized what he heard. "He is at the car. He's talking to his driver. He tells him they will go to the Iranian embassy in Damascus. The loyal army units have defeated the gang of deserters and Brotherhood fanatics who had the artillery battery. So be ready to go—"

"That's why the shellings quit," Gadgets commented.

" 'Are the electronics in the back?' 'Yes, sir.' He's not talking now; it sounds like he's opening the trunk... closing the trunk. He checked the electronics. His footsteps come to the seat, he sits down.... A man comes to talk to him, they talk about the rockets going through Tripoli and meeting the ship from Nicaragua, they're talking weather and travel time...."

Their hand-radios buzzed again. Gadgets pointed to

Blancanales; Blancanales nodded. As Gadgets listened to Akbar's whispered monologue and translation, Blancanales took Powell's report.

"It's a French diplomat. Some special representative from the Education Office."

"You planted the bug?"

"Most definitely, Pol. I'm listening to the French dipshit complaining to his driver about undisciplined Syrian soldiers. Didn't like us stopping them. Seems... says he'll complain to Colonel Dastgerdi himself. Is that interesting?"

"Continue monitoring," Blancanales told him. "We're monitoring a situation on this end. Radio us fast if something comes up."

"Will do."

Akbar looked at Gadgets. "He has left the car to go to the maps. I hear only noise now."

"That's all right." Gadgets concentrated, staring at a poster of the Ayatollah. "Oh, you old lunatic, I got a surprise for you. Oh, yeah!" Gadgets turned to his partners. "Time to go, dudes. We got a rude move to make!"

LONG LINES of military and civilian vehicles followed the curves of the highway through the mountains. Land Rovers, Japanese scout cars and Mercedes sedans risked head-on oblivion to pass the slow trucks and troop transports.

The Syrian army and air force had exterminated the last strongholds of the rebellion in the Shael mountains. With the end of the artillery and rocket barrages, the soldiers manning the checkpoints had finally released the hundreds of vehicles stalled by the war.

The document checks had not found the Americans. Via radio, Zhgenti had checked with the Syrian central command in the Bekaa. None of the officers at the major checkpoints reported the group of Americans. The Americans and their Shia militia allies had not stopped at a checkpoint or encountered a Syrian patrol. If Desmarais had told the truth, they remained somewhere in the Bekaa Valley, concealed by the storm and the chaos of the war.

Now Zhgenti raced east to Damascus. His unit, reinforced by Syrian soldiers and men from the Syrian intelligence service when political and military conditions allowed their reassignment, would take positions around the Iranian embassy, and there wait for the Americans to appear.

Despite his doubts, Zhgenti had finally agreed with Desmarais. The situation left him no choice. The Americans had outmaneuvered all the forces at his disposal— Soviet, Palestinian and Lebanese. Somewhere in the Bekaa, the Americans and their Shia allies attacked an Iranian target. Logically, after the strike, they would retreat to the west, where the coast allowed for transportation to Cyprus and their return to the United States.

But logic did not guide the Americans, not the usual logic of military planners. The American terror team slipped past expected targets, where prepared defenses awaited, to hit where no one had expected. Where concentric lines of defense ensured complete security from attack, they seemed to rise from the earth to kill and destroy.

This had been their technique throughout the two

years of operations. Zhgenti knew their record of successes. When the Egyptian wing of the fanatical Muslim Brotherhood, Soviet financed and armed, struck at a secret U.S. Air Force installation in Cairo, the American team had slashed through the cells of Islamic terror gangs. But they did not pursue the scattered individuals. Instead, they raced far into the Egyptian desert to martyr an entire garrison of Islamic warriors. In another campaign, they had parachuted into the mountains of Nicaragua and devastated a terror training camp. Then, only a day or two later, they had reappeared in Los Angeles to exterminate a terror unit preparing a binary nerve gas attack on the city.

With those Americans, Zhgenti could only expect the unexpected. Therefore, he had accepted the suggestion from Desmarais that he anticipate the illogical and establish a watch at the Iranian embassy.

Actually, when Zhgenti considered it, a certain logic suggested that the Americans would attack the embassy. They had tracked Iranians from Beirut to Mexico, then exterminated them. Now they attacked an Iranian base in the Bekaa.

So why not attack the Iranian embassy, the source of funding and guidance for the fanatics?

When the Americans came, Zhgenti would be there, waiting.

As his limousine ascended the ramp to street level, Colonel Dastgerdi saw the man known to his associates in UNESCO as Jean Pierre Giraud stride from the darkness. Dastgerdi pushed the button of his intercom.

"Driver, stop! That man comes with me."

"Yes, Colonel."

Throwing open the door, Dastgerdi greeted the man in French. But when the elegantly dressed United Nations functionary joined him in the Mercedes, Dastgerdi abandoned French and spoke in their native language, Russian.

"This is our night of victory, Comrade Suvorov," Dastgerdi announced, using the man's true name. "Another victory for the Special Forces of the Red Army!"

Suvorov feigned ignorance of Russian. He glanced to the bulletproof glass dividing their seats from the driver and continued in French. Dastgerdi laughed at his associate's concern.

"He cannot hear. The glass stops bullets and words. I am absolutely positive. Speak—it is a time for celebration." The Colonel opened the built-in bar, removed a bottle of vodka and filled two glasses. "After years, we can speak. We have overcome the technological limitations of our nation's weapons, overcome the ignorance of the Syrians and the stupidity of the Iranians. The American President will receive the reward of our struggles. To the inauguration!"

They gulped down the Russian alcohol. The limousine passed through the concentric rings of fencing protecting the rocket-development base. Dastgerdi looked out at the landscape of rock and snow. He laughed. "Never again will I see this miserable place. Now I can become an officer again! Forget your French, Suvorov! Speak our language."

"Is difficult to abandon caution," Suvorov admitted. "Speaking French and English, but never our tongue. Never allowing ourselves even to dream in our language, but . . . but for victory, it is nothing.''

As the Mercedes powered through the snow and ruts of the road to the highway, Dastgerdi poured two more shots of vodka. ''To the defeat of the old men—in Moscow and Washington. After the war, the Soviet army will rule all the world.''

The other Soviet laughed. ''But Syria and Iran and Iraq are not the world. We will gain the oil fields and the ports, three more socialist republics.''

''And it will be a victory for the army. Not the old men, not the KGB, not the diplomats. We will gain power over the Central Committee and then nothing can stop us. Nothing!''

''I do not believe we will push that far. The oil fields and the ports of the Gulf and Mediterranean, that is enough—''

''No! The world! Nothing less than the world!'' Dastgerdi splashed another shot into his glass. ''Victory for the Red Army! Victory for the special forces of the Soviet army intelligence service!''

As they neared the highway, the driver spoke through the intercom. ''Colonel Dastgerdi, a checkpoint. A group of our soldiers is blocking the road.''

''Drive past them!'' Dastgerdi told him. ''They have no authority to stop me.''

''Colonel, they have heavy weapons.''

The two Soviets looked out to see a heavy troop transport. Soldiers aimed a tripod-mounted 12.7mm machine gun at the Mercedes. Another soldier stood with a ready RPG launcher and rocket.

''I advise we stop,'' the driver concluded.

"Present our documents!" Dastgerdi ordered. "But I will not tolerate a delay."

Slowing to a stop, the driver rolled down his window. A Syrian soldier demanded their papers. Another tapped at the back window. The driver spoke through the intercom.

"They demand to search the car, Colonel."

"No! I will not allow it!" Throwing open the door, Dastgerdi attempted to step out. The muzzles of Kalashnikov rifles stopped him. Soldiers looked into the back.

"Your papers!" one of the Syrians ordered.

"Where is your officer?" Dastgerdi shouted.

"My officer is dead, killed by traitors in the uniforms of officers. Perhaps you are another traitor. Show us your papers. If you fight, we execute you."

With a rifle at his head, the driver walked to the trunk and unlocked it. Then the soldier pushed him back into the front seat.

Colonel Dastgerdi waited in the Mercedes limousine, raging at the stupidity of common soldiers.

17

Standing behind the truck, his pockets full of tools, Gadgets watched the driver open the trunk of the limousine. A Shia in a Syrian army uniform escorted the driver back to the front of the Mercedes. When the driver's door closed, Gadgets crossed the road to the open trunk.

The raised trunk lid blocked the view of the two men in the back seat. The trunk light illuminating his search, Gadgets opened the top suitcase. Clothes. Slipping his hands into the folded shirts and pants, he found nothing unusual. He put the suitcase aside and opened another.

Ten black plastic units, each the size of an AM transistor radio, lay cushioned on precut blocks of foam. He had no time to study or test them. He knew the purpose and the function of the units. Now he had to modify one.

Using the point of a watchmaker's screwdriver, he snapped open one of the black plastic cases. He saw circuit boards, components, hundreds of expertly soldered connections. Studying the components, he thumbed the power switch. A tiny red diode light on the side of the case glowed. The homing-impulse transmitter gave no other indication of operation.

Gadgets poked the screwdriver into the fine wires and separated the two leads to the switch. With micro-cutters, he snipped the wires from the switch, stripped off a few millimeters of insulation, then twisted the wires together. With a bit of black electrical tape he had stuck to his left thumbnail, he covered the twist in the wires.

Next, he found the two tiny wires leading to the red diode. He snipped the wires to kill the light. A second bit of tape secured the cut wires to the plastic case.

Closing the plastic case, Gadgets glanced to the nearest Shia, who maintained his impassive expression as his eyes flicked to Gadgets. Gadgets took a few more seconds and slipped a minimicrophone-transmitter into the suitcase of directional transmitters, jamming it deep between the foam padding and the suitcase shell.

He closed the case of electronics, returned it exactly where he found it, then replaced the suitcase on top. Signaling the Shia, Gadgets walked away without looking back. The Shia slammed the trunk lid closed.

Spinning its tires on the ice, exhaust clouding in the darkness, the limousine continued away. The taillights swayed as the vehicle bumped over the road, then the red points went over a rise and disappeared.

"All right!" Gadgets jumped into the air and slapped his hands together. "Did it, dudes! I did it. Fifteen thousand points on the pinball machine of foreign policy for the unknown Mr. Wizard!"

"Convoy coming!" Powell shouted. "Troop truck first in the line."

"Wizard!" Lyons ran to Gadgets. "Quit the cheer-leader routine. We got the guns in this truck. Come on.'' Lyons climbed into the back of the troop transport. He reached down to help his partner up. "What did you see in there?"

"I deserve some cheers! You don't know what I just did, you don't know the perfect justice of it. Remember what I said in Nicaragua about keeping your technology straight? Well, that Dasto just got his twisted."

Lyons slapped his gloved hands together in perfunctory applause as he took his place behind the Browning. "I know what you did. Now tell me what you saw."

"I saw the best electronics and ni-cad batteries that money can buy, that's what."

Gadgets sat down behind the MK-19 full-auto 40mm machine gun. The headlights of the approaching convoy lit the flakes of falling snow. Though they had their backs to the convoy, both Americans raised their collars to cover their faces.

"And everything I saw," Gadgets continued, "was stamped, Made in the USA."

"What?"

"No shit." Gadgets told him, putting valved hearing protectors into his ears. "Everything I saw I've got in my catalogs at home. I didn't see anything ComBloc, nothing that I didn't know about. So we know where the Syrian got his electronics—the US of A."

Squeaking and rattling announced the arrival of the Syrian troop transport. Behind the transport, a line of diesel trucks and trailers slowed. Each of the four trucks pulled two flatbed trailers carrying the shipping containers. There were a total of eight containers. Engines revved as the trucks slowed.

Behind the Browning, Lyons squatted and peered

through the slats at the Syrians. He pressed the transmit of his hand-radio. "Pol, you ready?"

"Loaded and locked," Blancanales answered.

"Ready here." Lyons pocketed his radio.

In the road, the Shias checked the transit documents presented by the Syrian officer in command of the platoon.

Behind the transport, in the clouds of diesel smoke and the glare of the headlights, other Shias moved in step with the plan. They went to the truck and trailer rigs and stepped up on the sides of the cabs. When the drivers opened the doors for the search, the Shias waved flashlights inside. Then the flashlights went out. Lyons did not see the Shias step down from the cabs. The doors closed.

A Shia ran to the Syrian transport. He saluted his Soviet advisor and the Soviet—Powell—waved the Syrians on. The driver revved the engine and engaged the gears.

Lyons stood up behind the Browning. Gadgets straightened a link in the belt of 40mm grenades. The Syrian troop transport bumped past the checkpoint and continued to the rise.

The line of trucks and trailers did not move.

A hundred meters past the checkpoint, the troop transport stopped. Powell shouted to the three men of Able Team, "Hit them!"

Heavy weapon reports shattered the night. Lyons held down the firing button of the Browning, firing full-auto .50-caliber into the soldiers crowded into the back of the trailer. The first high-explosive-and-white-phosphorous 40mm grenades hit an instant later. Blancanales scored several perfect shots into the back of the transport. Gadgets's first three grenades hit under the transport.

The Syrian soldiers died instantly, .50-caliber slugs passing through them without slowing, continuing through the sheet metal of the cab to kill the driver and officer. Exploding grenades slashed the dead and dying with thousands of steel-wire razors, the chemical fire of the white phosphorous igniting their flesh and uniforms, their munitions, the diesel fuel of the truck.

"Stop! Stop!" Powell shouted. The heavy weapons went silent. Unslinging a Kalashnikov, Powell ran to the burning truck. He circled the wreck, crouching as ammunition popped. One scream came from the cab. Powell sighted into the flames and triggered a quick burst. Then he ran back to the Americans and Shias.

"That's it, gentlemen," Powell yelled. "The rockets are now ours!"

Gadgets jumped from behind the grenade launcher, ran back to the trailers. Lyons and Powell followed. Shias opened the doors of the four trucks and threw out the bodies of the Syrian drivers.

Climbing up on a container in one of the trailers, Gadgets checked the bolts along the roof. Then he worked his way to the front of the container. He saw Lyons and Powell standing below him.

"Whoever designed all this had his act together. Supersimple. Unscrew the wing nuts on those bolts, then unlatch this thing here and the roof comes off. If you're going, say, sixty miles an hour, you can just eject the roof. They must've spent years working out all the technical details on this hit."

"You checking the rockets?" Lyons shouted over the noise of the idling diesel engines.

"I'll check the rockets, you get this convoy ready to move. Faster we move, more chance we'll make our score."

"What about the base?" Powell asked. "Thought you came here to hit it."

Lyons laughed. "After this, the Syrians... they'll bomb it. They'll bring bulldozers and bury it. Anything to cover up the evidence."

In A ZIL LIMOUSINE borrowed from the Soviet embassy, Zhgenti and Desmarais watched the Iranian embassy, one short block away. Other vehicles—military trucks, unmarked civilian cars, panel trucks—served as observation posts for his men on other streets. And behind the walls of a vacant mansion in this quarter of French colonial-period estates, two platoons of Syrian commandos waited in reserve.

The military vehicles would not appear suspicious. On this night of rebellion and chaotic warfare, Syrian security units had taken positions everywhere in the city. No common people braved the streets. Soldiers maintained martial peace in the Syrian capital.

"If the Americans come," Zhgenti said, "they die."

"*When* they come!" Desmarais countered. "Not *if*. I am sure."

"You are so familiar with them that you can foretell their moves?"

"They are ruthless killers, death-squad goons. They have no restraints. Their government does not control them. They do as they will. If they came to kill Iranians, they will come to the embassy. They care nothing for international law or the rights of diplomats, they will—"

"The Iranians?" Zhgenti asked, confused by her impassioned diatribe.

"No! The fascists! The Americans! But their own lust for murder will betray them, lead them into the trap we've set."

"If they come..." Zhgenti commented. "And do you still have your camera? You can record our victory for the newspapers of the world."

"Yes, here. I hope it still works." She slipped the expensive camera from her shoulder, removed the lens cap, looked through the viewfinder, tested the batteries, turned the focus and f-stop rings. "Somehow, after everything I've gone through tonight, it still operates. But if they come before dawn, it will be useless."

Zhgenti smiled. "For you, just for you, my little Canadian—"

"Quebecois!" Desmarais corrected.

"Oh, yes! As a gesture of socialist comradeship, I will order the Syrians to fire white flares. To light the night for the record of history. The photos will be important for the newspapers. And as Lenin said, 'The press is the greatest weapon of socialism.' Good, yes? He understood the value of stories and photos. But I think we will have long to wait."

They sat in silence for a few minutes, watching the lights of the Iranian embassy. In response to the political and religious crisis in Syria, the Iranians had assembled all their staff, all the consuls and attaches, on the grounds of the embassy. The Syrian intelligence service had told Zhgenti that the Iranians denied any part in the fundamentalist assault on the Assad regime. But in response to Syrian surveillance, the Iranians put out a call for all the Iranian diplomatic corps to gather within their embassy.

As Zhgenti and Desmarais watched, vehicles arrived. But none left.

Bored and tired, knowing his men and the Syrian agents also waited for the Americans, Zhgenti relaxed. He watched the Canadian woman watching for the men she hoped to see die.

A very pretty woman. Also a traitor to her country and an enemy to all North Americans. When the Soviet Union took the Americas, she would be among the first to die. International socialism needed no whores like her, selling out her country for expense accounts and free airline tickets.

But a very pretty woman. And willing to do things of interest to a man. A shameless woman. He had seen what she did with that rich Arab, that Muslim warlord with a limousine.

Now Zhgenti had a limousine. Would she do the same for him? He hadn't had a woman since last week in Bulgaria. That woman had been an honest whore, but not very attractive, exhausted by years of caring alone for her children after her husband was executed by the KGB. Rejected by her family, the widow had turned to part-time prostitution to buy her children a few hard-currency gifts—good shoes, textbooks, a few tins of meat for the holidays.

An honest prostitute. But not as pretty as this woman who sat with him now.

"Frenchie," Zhgenti said to Desmarais. "How did you get away from the Americans? Show me."

"What?"

"It will pass the time."

"What are you talking about?"

"Like in that other limousine—"

Desmarais reached for the door handle. Zhgenti grabbed her arm and jerked her closer. His thick lips touched the smooth, soft skin of her face.

"You want a bad report to our superiors? You play a very tricky game, my little Canadian. All your lies, all your ways of lying. Perhaps they will terminate your contract. Perhaps they will issue instructions for me to terminate your contract. Or perhaps I will terminate you immediately, and then explain. You have your choice. Do like you did for the Arab."

She did.

As the night unfolded, Zhgenti enjoyed her three more times. Finally, exhausted, only one eye open to watch her, his right hand secure on the pistol in his coat pocket, Zhgenti compared the technique of the Canadian to the pleasures of the middle-aged Bulgarian prostitute.

Rather automatic and mechanical and cold.

Like her lies.

18

"I thought that diplomat was French!" Gadgets shouted over the wind and engine roar in the back of the Mercedes troop transport.

After the hijacking, Gadgets had returned to his equipment to find ten minutes of Russian on his voice-activated cassette recorder. The conversation between the French diplomat and the Syrian colonel began in Arabic, went to French, then turned exclusively to Russian.

Now, huddled amid crates of ammunition and contraband, Gadgets monitored Colonel Dastgerdi and the French diplomat as they conversed in Russian on the road to the Syrian capital of Damascus.

Five kilometers behind their limousine, Able Team and the Shias followed in a convoy of military vehicles and four hijacked cargo trucks. Other convoys jammed the highway as the Syrian army rushed wounded soldiers from the Bekaa Valley to Damascus in empty munitions trucks. Trucks laden with weapons and munitions labored in the opposite direction to resupply the forces still fighting in the Bekaa.

Desperate to expedite the flow of men and munitions between the several rebellion hotspots, the Syrian army waved Able Team's convoy through checkpoints after only quick glances at the drivers and their documents. Following the limousine of Colonel Dastgerdi, Able Team maintained a relentless pace to Damascus.

Gadgets shouted across the back of the troop transport, "Didn't Mr. Marine say that the diplomat in the limo had French identification?"

"I'll check." Lyons took out his hand-radio.

Gadgets continued monitoring and taping the dialogue in the limousine. Though he did not understand the Russian, he would save the tape for translation.

"Yeah!" Lyons confirmed. "A French diplomat. Works for UNESCO. Name of J. P. Gee-Road."

"Oh, man, this shit never quits."

"What?"

"Use your radio!" Gadgets yelled, holding up his hand-radio. "I want Mr. Marine to monitor this jive. Beep-beep, come in Cowboy Radio Network, this is the Wizard broadcasting another mystery."

"What're you talking about?" Powell, riding at the head of the convoy in the Land Rover, had to shout over the road noise.

"This is it," Gadgets began. "We got a mystery. It ain't a Syrian and a Frenchie in that limo, it's two Russians. In—"

"How do you know?" Powell asked.

"They're talking Russian. Now listen, in Mexico City, Illovich of the KGB didn't know nothing of the Iranians and the rockets. Then Desmarais—if we can believe anything she says—told us that a KGB kill squad had been assigned to track us down and wipe us out. And since Desmarais knows we came here to hit the gang making the rockets, we can assume the KGB knows what we came to do. So here's the question. Who are those Russians in the limo? If they were KGB, the KGB wouldn't have a kill squad chasing us. They'd have gone out to that factory base and waited for us to show up. They're not KGB because Illovich in Mexico would've known—or could've found out—all about what's going on. So who are they?''

Blancanales joined the electronic conversation. Sheltered by boxes of Italian designer jeans, he spoke into his radio. ''What do you think?''

''Me?'' Gadgets answered. ''Me, think? I don't know what to think! That's why I'm asking the questions!''

''Marine?'' Blancanales used Powell's informal code name despite the encrypting circuits of the NSA hand-radios they used. ''Do any of our Shia friends speak or understand Russian?''

''Not that I know of.''

''Then save the tapes, Wizard.'' Blancanales concluded. ''We'll know later.''

''I hate the suspense. Could be something important to the—''

''Forget it,'' Lyons interrupted. ''Those two in the limo are dead. What they say is history.''

SOVIET TANKS AND ARMORED PERSONNEL CARRIERS controlled every major intersection in Damascus. In the limousine, Dastgerdi and Suvorov looked out at streets and boulevards populated only by soldiers. No citizens risked the streets.

Soldiers at checkpoints stopped the limousine every few blocks. After the third checkpoint, to save himself the bother of continually opening and closing his window, the driver left the window open and held the necessary papers. Officers glanced at the documents, then peered at the Syrian colonel and French diplomat. The succession of checkpoints enraged Dastgerdi.

"These Syrians! Searching my car, checking my papers! Do I look like a mullah?"

Finally they drove through the tree-lined avenues of the French colonial quarter to the embassy of the Islamic Republic of Iran. There, at the ornate wrought-iron gates, Revolutionary Guards stopped the limousine.

"This completes our plan," Dastgerdi said to Suvorov. "From embassy to the factory to the rockets, the trail of evidence is complete. We will visit with our friends, then be gone. To watch for the televised glories of our achievement."

Half-asleep with fatigue and vodka, Suvorov only nodded.

A bearded, tangle-haired Guard motioned for Dastgerdi to leave the limousine. Cursing under his breath, the colonel opened the door. He presented the handwritten note from Mohammed Ayat with the seal of Iran identifying him as one of the faithful.

The Guards glanced at the note. Talking to one another and staring at Colonel Dastgerdi, they opened the gate. Inside, Dastgerdi saw bumper-to-bumper limousines on the driveways. Islamic militiamen slept on the immaculate lawns. At the front of the old French mansion, mullahs and diplomats and functionaries crowded the entry and reception room.

"How long shall I tell the attendants that we will be here?" the driver asked.

"Stay with the car," Dastgerdi told him through the intercom. "We will leave soon. I will take my case, my friend Giraud."

Suvorov, returning to his role as the French diplomat Jean Pierre Giraud, paused to straighten his clothes. Colonel Dastgerdi took the suitcase containing the ten homing-impulse transmitters from the limousine's trunk.

Revolutionary Guards and soon-to-be exiled mullahs of the defeated Muslim Brotherhood stared at the hated uniform of Syria that Dastgerdi wore. But then one of the elegant Iranians, Mohammed Ayat, attaché of the faithful, rushed out and embraced Dastgerdi.

In his mind, as Ayat's arms closed around him, Dastgerdi rejoiced. All the onlookers would remember his reception. They would tell others. After the rocket attack, the embrace of a Syrian colonel by an Iranian functionary would be one more link in the damning chain of evidence.

They entered the embassy.

"THAT WAS COLONEL DASTGERDI!" Desmarais exclaimed, pointing at the limousine entering the gates of the Iranian embassy.

"Take a picture." Zhgenti kept his hand on the pistol in his pocket. He knew the woman hated him. Perhaps she hoped to trick him. Forcing her to service him had been unprofessional and self-indulgent. For the thrill of car-seat sex, he must now watch for her revenge.

"The Americans will be here soon. They probably followed him. In Mexico, they used directional finding devices. They may or may not attack the embassy, but they are close. I am sure of that.''

''Stop talking and go. Go!''

Without another word, Desmarais stepped into the frigid predawn air. Zhgenti waited until she had walked a hundred meters, then stepped out into the cold. He took a few deep breaths to clear his wits. Then he opened the driver's door and sat down behind the wheel. The interior of the Zil limousine stank.

Zhgenti started the engine. He watched Desmarais pause and look up and down the dark avenue. She fitted a flash unit onto the camera, then retreated to the shadows to await the Americans.

Does she think she can escape when the Americans come? Will she, Zhgenti wondered, tell them about Soviet foreign operations in exchange for escape?

Gunning the engine, Zhgenti waited and watched. He put the Uzi submachine gun on the seat beside him. He would not let her escape.

That trick she would not repeat.

ELEVEN KILOMETERS FROM THE IRANIAN EMBASSY, Powell signaled the drivers of the cargo trucks to stop. The heavy trucks and trailers parked along the shoulder. Last in the convoy, the driver of the troop transport set the lights blinking.

As the military traffic continued past, Lyons and Blancanales ran forward to Powell, their Soviet greatcoats catching the wind. Gadgets stayed to monitor the conversation in Dastgerdi's limousine.

Powell spread a map of Damascus on the hood of the

Land Rover. With a compass, he plotted the direction to the Iranian embassy.

"This stretch isn't dead on," he told Lyons and Blancanales. "But ahead, before we get to Dadsaya, the road's got the correct orientation."

"What's the distance from ground zero?" Lyons asked.

"By this map, ten . . . maybe ten point one clicks. Better to be short than long, right?"

"I guess. All this traffic. . . ." Lyons glanced at the passing transports. "One truck stalls, it's going to delay the launch."

Blancanales looked at the hijacked diesels. "Why is there a difference if they're in motion or parked?"

"The tops, man. If. . ." Powell started. Taking out his hand-radio, he buzzed Gadgets. "Mr. Gizmo. Think it makes a difference if the trucks are moving when the rockets take off?"

"Why?" Gadgets asked.

"Yeah, why? Forget it, gentlemen. The Red Army parks their rocket launchers, why not us?"

"I only figured on a moving blast-off because the crazies planned on that," Gadgets said. "Why don't we pull off the lids? If the road ain't right, it's park and shoot."

Powell nodded. "You got it. What're you monitoring?"

"They're in Damascus. Don't know exactly where or doing what. Akbar's listening in. But it's all Ruskie talk."

"We'll pull off the tops as soon as—"

"Hey!" The hand-radios carried Gadgets's enthusiasm to them. "Akbar says they're talking Arabic. They're in the Iranian embassy. Undo those wing nuts! It's blast-off time!"

"The Wizard does it again," Lyons commented.

"What?" Blancanales asked.

"All those bolts and nuts?" Lyons looked at the roof of the nearest truck. "In this cold, we work with the hardware while the Wizard listens to his radios."

Then Lyons climbed onto the truck and twisted off the first fastener. All the other men joined him, working quickly in the cold before dawn.

THE FIRST LIGHT OF DAWN GLOWED in the east. In the office of Mohammed Ayat, Dastgerdi and Suvorov, the latter maintaining his role of French diplomat, examined the ten homing-impulse transmitters. On the polished walnut top of the desk, beside the intricate silver repoussé of the lid of an ancient Persian dish, the black plastic units looked futuristic, alien.

"So small!" Ayat mused. "Are you certain—"

"I am certain!" Dastgerdi stated. "I have no doubts. The design incorporates the most modern technology available. Every component has been tested and retested. Giraud's agents need only activate the transmitters and wait—"

"For death." The Iranian flicked the switch of a unit. The red light came on. He flicked the switch off. "How simple. They do not even know of their martyrdom. Very simple. Eliminates the necessity for the indoctrination required in our efforts. Very tiresome, the endless lectures and prayers that the village boys of Iran require before they embrace the concept of martyrdom. Your way is much more expedient."

"From the first," Dastgerdi explained, "I have known that we could not plan on volunteers—expendables—to carry the transmitters. Not volunteers who knew their purpose."

As he spoke, he returned the units to the cut foam, adjusting and readjusting them. After this meeting, the homing-impulse transmitters left his possession and became the responsibility of Suvorov, alias Giraud, who would transport and distribute them in Washington, District of Columbia.

"That is because, first, of the relations between your nation and the United States. And second, I could not depend on a volunteer. Volunteers can change their minds, lose their faith."

He touched an object between the foam and the plastic shell of the carrying case, and by touch discerned its form: a disk of metal, with the diameter of a coin but several times the thickness. He bent back the foam and glanced at the disk. One side had a smooth surface, the other coarse, like the covering of a—

Microphone.

"Yes," Ayat remembered. "We had that problem with the driver of a truck into the Marine barracks. He remained fervent in his desire for martyrdom until the time came for his drive to Paradise. In that case, we resorted to drugs. That is, I am told: of course, I know nothing of that. It was the action of the Islamic Jihad...."

For Dastgerdi, the Iranian's words receded, as if he had spoken from a great distance. The words, the project, the plot meant nothing now.

Without emotion, from a gray place of training and intellect, Dastgerdi contemplated his defeat.

Somewhere, somehow, the Americans or the KGB had infiltrated his project. But where? *The checkpoint.* There, nowhere else, could they have placed the microphone.

His mind turned, methodically analyzing this revelation. Touching the microphone, his hand covered by the foam padding, he considered his options. Immediate flight? No. Soviet or American, they would be near. Destroy the microphone?

But as he touched the microphone, he realized the plot had not yet failed. He had worked with all the spy devices available to Soviet agents. Soviet technology offered KGB agents nothing so small, so ingenious.

Americans had manufactured the device and placed it.

Americans now listened to Ayat brag of murdering hundreds of United States Marines.

Though the rockets would never rain down on the inauguration, agents of the CIA would be waiting when Palestinians and Nicaraguans transferred the rockets to an American ship crewed by American black nationalists. An army of FBI agents would wait for the couriers to pass the homing devices to the ten expendables with invitations to the inauguration.

The President would not die in a rain of doom.

But the people of the United States would receive a prime-time television briefing on the plot, with irrefutable evidence—rockets, transmitters, agents—''

And tape recordings of this meeting in the Iranian embassy.

Dastgerdi left the microphone in the case.

''This will be another glory to the name of the Islamic Jihad,'' Dastgerdi told the Iranian.

"A glory for Iran and Syria," Ayat added.

"Oh, yes," Dastgerdi continued. He knew his words would soon emanate from millions of American television sets, in the Arabic he spoke and in simultaneous translation. He spoke for history. "Of course. The assassination of the President of the United States, the head of Satan's regime on earth, the slaughter of the filthy writhing snakes attending his evil ceremonial inauguration. Our nations shall share the harvest of this triumph of our faith."

"Insallah," Ayat added.

A harvest of war and destruction and Soviet dominion.

19

As the sky lightened with dawn, Anne Desmarais stamped her numb feet in the gateway of the embassy of the People's Democratic Republic of Korea. The North Korean sentries stared at her from their guard positions, gloved hands on Kalashnikov rifles. The Soviets had notified their Korean comrades of the surveillance of the Iranian embassy. The North Koreans cooperated by not shooting the Canadian woman loitering outside their gates.

Desmarais watched the Iranian gate, and intermittently scanned the long tree-shadowed avenue, noting the surveillance vehicles—a panel truck at one end, Zhgenti's Zil limousine at the other—and the cars passing infrequently on the distant boulevard. She went through the motions of her charade as a photojournalist, holding the camera, watching for subjects, maintaining her position in the shadows and her demeanor as the calm professional.

But the taste of Zhgenti's semen was still in her mouth and her mind raged with shame and hatred. The hours of degradation in the limousine as she fulfilled his crude demands now twisted her reason and filled her vision with scenes of bullets punching his squat body, of high explosives spilling out his guts, of fire charring his face. . . .

With the help of the Americans, Zhgenti would die. She knew they would come. And when they did, she would point out the Soviet hit man waiting to kill them. They would reward her with forgiveness for her past work with the Soviets. Perhaps she would become an agent for the Americans.

Would the Americans capture Zhgenti? He knew many details of KGB operations throughout Europe and the Middle East. Would they torture him? Would they allow her to watch? Would they allow her to guide their tortures, to allow their tortures to become her revenge?

Zhgenti would pay for degrading her: first with high voltage through clamped-on electrodes, then with cuts from razor blades, then with chemicals rubbed into the slashes, then shocks, slashes, and again chemical burns....

Until only a bleeding, pus-flowing ruin would remain. The roar of an explosion shattered her thoughts. Then the dawn exploded in unending blasts of high explosive as flashes tore the street, threw walls into the air, shattered the mansions of the quarter. Fragments of steel sang past her, ricochetting off stone and the wrought-iron gates. Then debris—stone, wood, flesh, glass—showered the street. Screams came from the grounds of the Iranian embassy as the maimed and dying felt their wounds.

Artillery! Panic seized Desmarais. She ran from the shelter of the North Korean gate.

Then the next salvo of rockets rained down.

TERROR DESCENDED ON THE IRANIANS. Roaring flames and shock waves tore apart the embassy and the grounds, the explosions coming too quickly to count or differentiate; the upper floor of the old French neo-roccoco mansion disintegrated; limousines in the curving drive disappeared in storms of light and spinning scrap metal; a group of running Guards melted in the blast; all this in the first strike of twenty-four rockets.

Twisted metal fell from the sky as sections of trucks and limousines crashed onto the pavement. Wood and plaster hammered the embassy and the grounds. Thousands of bits of unidentifiable debris rained down in the long second after the chain of explosions.

The mullahs in their blood-crimson robes stared at the anatomical displays sprayed on still-standing walls and trees, only detached arms and legs and intestines and raw pink meat remaining of those who had been closest to the explosions. Revolutionary Guards, in shock, attempted to rise from the floor to fulfill their responsibilities, only to discover their legs gone, or their skulls opened, or sections of lumber protruding from their chests.

A chemical odor overwhelmed the stink of blood and excrement and explosives. The yellow gas swirled through the ceiling and walls, drifted across the wreckage and corpses and wounded on the stately lawns.

The remains of limousines flamed. Chemical fire blazed. Points of white phosphorous glowed on corpses. Stunned wounded thrashed at the white fire burning their bodies. White phosphorous sparkled in the boughs of the trees like stars, burning through leaves and twigs to drop to other branches.

The shattered mansion creaked and sagged, floors

and ceilings falling, walls tottering, crystal smashing and silver ringing as cabinets fell. Ammunition popped in the flaming hulks of the limousines and trucks.

As the debris settled, an instant of silence followed. Those who still lived heard ragged breathing. Having suffered the traumatic amputation of a hand, a Guard reached for his Kalashnikov, the twin jagged bones of his forearm scratching across the stamped-steel receiver of the autorifle. Then footsteps and prayers broke the silence as survivors scrambled through the wreckage and gore, attempting to escape the horror.

Sprawled on the asphalt of the drive, the flames from the burning vehicles scorching his face, Colonel Dastgerdi stared at the destruction around him.

The Syrians had gone insane! Dastgerdi raged. Shelling an embassy! Even if Iran had conspired against the regime, even if they provided sanctuary for the defeated fanatics of the Muslim Brotherhood. . . .

He saw his suitcase of electronics a few steps away. The hand and arm of Jean Pierre Giraud, still in the sleeve of his tailored jacket, held the handle. Dastgerdi saw only the hand and arm. Giraud had disappeared.

Dastgerdi tried to rise. Pain stopped him. Clawing at the asphalt, he reached the suitcase and threw away the dead hand. He tried to crawl away with the suitcase, but he could not. Only one leg responded; the other was numb. He looked down and saw a piece of steel protruding from it.

The barrel-and-piston assembly of a Kalashnikov had impaled his leg: not a fatal wound. He could continue. Determined to survive, determined to forward the transmitters to the United States where the units would become props in the elaborate national media trial and condemnation of Iran, Dastgerdi crawled away from the flames.

Yellow mist enveloped him: he smelled dichlorethyl sulphide and clamped his jaw. A breath would draw the blistering poison mist, otherwise known as mustard gas, into his lungs. Struggling not to panic, not to breathe, Dastgerdi flailed at the asphalt, trying to somehow drag himself and the precious transmitter units away.

Then he looked up and saw his rain of doom.

In an instant of stopped-time vision, he saw the converging rockets descending. The 240mm rockets, traveling at five hundred meters a second, appeared to float for the instant of recognition.

Dastgerdi realized the truth: his own rockets fell from the gray sky, the transmitters in the suitcase he held guiding them and their deadly warheads to the place where he lay wounded and immobile and exposed on the driveway pavement.

The vision passed and then came the rockets. Shrapnel ripped over him, severing an ear, taking away a leg, throwing him through the mist. Finally he screamed and, drawing another breath, filled his lungs with chemical death. He screamed again and again, his one voice of terror lost in the roar.

ZHGENTI KNEW THE SOUND OF KATYUSHAS. Throwing the Zil into gear, he floored the accelerator. But the heavy limousine seemed to move no faster than a walk, the acceleration taking him away from the curb but not gaining the speed his desperation needed. His plight reminded him of a dreadful scene in a nightmare; he could not escape the barrage.

Debris showered the Zil, clanging on the hood and roof, tumbling away. Zhgenti kept the accelerator to the floor.

Far ahead, Desmarais ran from the gateway. What role did she have in this attack, this strike by rockets? Zhgenti knew she had some devious involvement. She would not escape. He aimed the limousine at the journalist who had served the Soviet Union, using the five-pointed star of the hood ornament to sight on her body.

"No more tricks, my little Canadian!"

Explosions flashed as another rain of rockets fell on the Iranian embassy. Window glass sprayed the interior of the Zil. The shock slammed Zhgenti, and he felt his ears ringing with agony. But he did not lose control of the limousine.

Focusing his eyes, he saw Desmarais. Camera in hand, her lustrous hair flagging in the wind, she sat on the hood of the Zil.

Zhgenti laughed. Desmarais did not sit. What remained of her was in front of him, impaled on the unseen hood ornament.

"You did not escape, not this time. . . ."

FLAME AND SILENCE. Desmarais felt the blast lift her above the street. She floated for an infinite moment—the dawn sky wheeling, the flashes of high-explosive flame spinning past, noise coming and receding—then fell. Something struck her and she ran.

She did not feel her legs pumping, but she knew she sprinted because the asphalt of the avenue blurred and scenes of destruction flashed past. The thunder of the blasts continued, but in an instant she left the explosions behind.

She realized she still had her camera in her hands. Secured by the strap around her neck and gripped tightly in both hands, the camera had not been lost. She turned—so effortlessly, so quickly—to take a photo of the destruction behind her.

Zhgenti was mocking her. Through a shattered windshield, she saw his thick features sneering and laughing. She saw the steering wheel in his hands. Zhgenti was driving the limousine.

But I am running, she thought. I am escaping.... I will be free of Zhgenti and the Soviet monsters....

How could I be running? The explosion threw me onto the hood of the car. That is why I'm moving so fast.... Will Zhgenti take me to safety? Why is Zhgenti laughing?

Finally looking down, she saw the answer. Her body ended at her waist. Replacing her pelvis and legs, she saw the polished black hood of the Zil limousine.

Streams of blood showed at the union between her body and the gleaming metal of the Soviet limousine.

Her throat constricted to scream, her diaphragm contracted to expel that scream but instead released a vast gush of blood from her transected abdomen and she lost consciousness, her vision of the dawn going black.

Eyes fluttering, her face up to the sky, her hair flagging back, the young woman raced away from the maelstrom of death on the polished black enamel of the Soviet limousine. Even in the final rushing moments of her life, her dark hair and pale features graced the obsolete mechanical contradictory symbol of Soviet luxury—

As a hood ornament.

Missiles destroy Iranian embassy
Unknown forces claim responsibility

BEIRUT (AutoMagInt)—At dawn today, missiles destroyed the embassy of Iran in Damascus. Syrian state radio, monitored in Beirut, reported that the attack had also heavily damaged the embassies of the People's Democratic Republic of Korea (North Korea) and the People's Democratic Republic of Yemen.

Owing to the continuing sectarian fighting in Syria and the Bekaa Valley between forces loyal to President Hafez Assad and rebellious army units demanding an Islamic state, journalists based here could not confirm the conflicting reports of chemical weapons employed in the attack. However, sources that asked not to be named told of rescue workers withdrawing from the scene with blistered hands and severe respiratory distress.

The embassies of North Korea and Marxist Yemen could not be reached by telephone.

Iranian national radio denounced Syrian President Hafez Assad for "his vicious attack on the sovereign grounds of our embassy."

Sources in Beirut and Tripoli would not comment on the accusations of Syrian complicity in the barrage.

In Beirut, a caller speaking for a previously unknown group claimed responsibility for the attack. Speaking in idiomatic American English, the caller stated, "The Cowboy Jihad righteously wasted that gang of crazies. We'll never forget October 23, 1983. Tell the mullahs, you can run and you can hide, but the posse of the apocalypse rides in the night. The payback won't quit till we kill talkshit Khomeini!"

MORE GREAT ACTION
COMING SOON

#17 Fire and Maneuver
PROSECUTION TO THE MAX!

The hardcore vets of Able Team hunt a
vicious killer and find themselves caught
up in an explosive all-or-nothing war
between two rival drug syndicates in the
steaming Colombian jungle.

The Team is on a search-and-destroy mission,
and that means death for everyone.

Mack Bolan's

ABLE TEAM

by Dick Stivers

Action writhes in the reader's own street as Able Team's Carl "Mr. Ironman" Lyons, Pol Blancanales and Gadgets Schwarz make triple trouble in blazing war. To these superspecialists, justice is as sharp as a knife. Join the guys who began it all—Dick Stivers's Able Team!

"This guy has a fertile mind and a great eye for detail. Dick Stivers is brilliant!"

—*Don Pendleton*

GOLD
EAGLE

**Nile Barrabas and the
Soldiers of Barrabas are the**

SOBs

by Jack Hild

Nile Barrabas is a nervy son of a bitch who was the last
American soldier out of Vietnam and the first man into a
new kind of action. His warriors, called the Soldiers of
Barrabas, have one very simple ambition: to do what the
Marines can't or won't do. Join the Barrabas blitz! Each
book hits new heights—this is brawling at its best!

"Nile Barrabas is one tough SOB himself.... A wealth of
detail.... SOBs does the job!"
                                   —*West Coast Review of Books*

#1 The Barrabas Run   #4 Show No Mercy
#2 The Plains of Fire   #5 Gulag War
#3 Butchers of Eden

GOLD
EAGLE

Available wherever paperbacks are sold.

GET THE NEW WAR BOOK AND MACK BOLAN BUMPER STICKER FREE!

Mail this coupon today!

FREE! THE NEW WAR BOOK AND MACK BOLAN BUMPER STICKER when you join our home subscription plan.

Gold Eagle Reader Service, a division of Worldwide Library
In U.S.A.: 2504 W. Southern Avenue, Tempe, Arizona 85282
In Canada: P.O. Box 2800, Postal Station A, 5170 Yonge Street, Willowdale, Ont. M2N 6J3

YES, rush me <u>The New War Book</u> and Mack Bolan bumper sticker FREE, and, under separate cover, my first six Gold Eagle novels. These first six books are mine to examine free for 10 days. If I am not entirely satisfied with these books, I will return them within 10 days and owe nothing. If I decide to keep these novels, I will pay just $1.95 per book (total $11.70). I will then receive the six Gold Eagle novels every other month, and will be billed the same low price of $11.70 per shipment. I understand that each shipment will contain two Mack Bolan novels, and one each from the Able Team, Phoenix Force, SOBs and Track libraries. There are no shipping and handling or any other hidden charges. I may cancel this arrangement at any time, and <u>The New War Book</u> and bumper sticker are mine to keep as gifts, even if I do not buy any additional books.

IMPORTANT BONUS: If I continue to be an active subscriber to Gold Eagle Reader Service, you will send me FREE, with every shipment, the AUTOMAG newsletter as a FREE BONUS!

Name	(please print)
Address	Apt. No.
City	State/Province Zip/Postal Code
Signature	(If under 18, parent or guardian must sign.)

This offer limited to one order per household. We reserve the right to exercise discretion in granting membership. If price changes are necessary you will be notified.

116-BPM-PAE5   AA-SUB-1F